ZOMBIE POWDER

SPELLS FOR HIRE BOOK TWO

STEFON MEARS

Thousand
Faces
Publishing

Also by Stefon Mears

Cavan Oltblood Series
Half a Wizard
The Ice Dagger
Spells of Undeath

Spells for Hire
Devil's Shoestring
Zombie Powder
Spirit Trap
Dragon's Blood (coming December 2019)

The Rise of Magic
Magician's Choice
Sleight of Mind
Lunar Alchemy
Three Fae Monte
The Sphinx Principle

The Telepath Trilogy
Surviving Telepathy
Immoral Telepathy
Targeting Telepathy

Edge of Humanity
Caught Between Monsters
Hunting Monsters

Power City Tales
Not Quite Bulletproof
No Money in Heroism

Devil's Night
Portal-Land, Oregon
Stealing from Pirates
Fade to Gold
With a Broken Sword
Twice Against the Dragon
The House on Cedar Street
Sudden Death
On the Edge of Faerie
Confronting Legends (Spells & Swords Vol. 1)
Uncle Stone Teeth and Other Macabre Poems
The Patreon Collection, Vol. 1-4 (Vol. 5, coming soon)

Published by Thousand Faces Publishing, Portland, Oregon

http://1kfaces.com

Copyright © 2018 by Stefon Mears

Front cover image © Dmitrijs Bindemanis | Dreamstime.com

This book was originally published as *The Price of Demons*.

ISBN-13: 978-1-948490-09-2

Zombie Powder

Spells for Hire | Book Two

AUTHOR'S NOTE

Spells for Hire stories take place in a world that is very like our own, but is not our own.

Thus, you might be able to visit some of the locations described in this book, such as the Witch's Castle in Forest Park. Others, however, have been fictionalized or invented whole cloth, like Gripper. Where I have fictionalized or invented, I have tried to maintain that unique Portland vibe.

In much the same way, religions such as Vodou, Candomblé and Shugendō exist in this world, as do other practices such as Hoodoo. I have done substantial research in my attempts to keep my portrayals true to the spirit of those beliefs and practices. I have, however, taken liberties for dramatic purposes. I hope that devotees of those religions and practices will forgive any mistakes I have made.

1

ONLY IN PORTLAND, OREGON, COULD HEATH CYR FIND A TASTE OF home off the back of a cart. Today that taste was shrimp étouffée, from a food cart called Ahnvee that specialized in Cajun cooking. Two or three of Portland's famous food carts served Cajun food, but Ahnvee was his favorite. They captured the flavors just right.

The lady who did the cooking for Ahnvee, Shawna, had a big, down-home smile too. Mind you, she was so white even her hair barely managed any yellow, but she had a touch of that Cajun drawl like she was from Louisiana herself. If a few years removed.

Not that Heath had any stones to throw about that. He barely remembered Louisiana from his own childhood and had only been back a few times. His mom and dad had moved their little family to New York before Heath was four years old, which meant he hadn't lived around New Orleans in over twenty years himself.

But the bits he remembered always made him smile. Wrought iron fences, blues and jazz everywhere like they were part of the air he breathed, and especially the food.

And this lunchtime meal under the bright blue August sky, it tasted just like his grandmother's shrimp étouffée. Shrimp and a little crab meat, a blond roux, and no tomatoes messing up the spices.

Tomatoes in cooking were like dragon's blood incense in conjuring — used right they were perfect, but used wrong they muddied up everything else. Both were best left out of étouffée altogether.

And this shrimp étouffée was the perfect thing to wash down with unsweetened iced tea on a hot Thursday afternoon, when the air had that just-right touch of humid cling to let you know it's there. New Orleans, Manhattan, Portland, everywhere Heath had lived, humid cling was always part of the summer air.

Altogether, the food and the day were almost enough to make Heath forget someone was trying to kill him.

Almost.

The threat had come only last night, in Gripper, the only bar worth going to for people walking one of the paths of magic. Heath had been drinking with a couple of *curanderos* who worked over on the east side of the Willamette River, comparing notes about the way they used High John the Conqueror in combination with Devil's Shoestring, when that saggy couch potato of a "Western Ceremonial Magician" who called himself Mandrake — Drake for short — stood and made his pronouncement.

Heath Cyr, for interfering in my business I condemn to you die. My demons will come for you.

Heath laughed of course. One of the few good things Heath had learned from his Uncle Andre was that the best public response to a death threat was laughter.

Long as you're calling up demons, Heath had answered, *you might want to have one see about that hairline of yours.*

That got people laughing, but not Maggie, of course. She was the Gripper's owner and a pretty major hand with Western Ceremonial Magic herself. And she did not abide death threats in her bar.

She hustled Drake out her red front door so fast he was almost flying. But then, Maggie was built like a boxer and could probably have hefted Drake over her head in a dead lift. Which meant she could have bench pressed a modestly built guy like Heath for twenty reps.

For violating the Gripper's death-threat policy — yes, it was common enough that they had an official policy — Drake wouldn't be allowed back in for at least a season. More likely a year and a day, because Maggie had a soft spot for Heath. Didn't matter, though. Drake'd accomplished what he wanted. The threat was made, and everyone who mattered in the Portland area had either heard it or would hear about it soon enough.

The entire occult community would be watching them both.

That was why the first thing Heath did on getting up late the next morning — after a couple of petitions for some protection — was make sure he was seen eating downtown, smiling like he didn't have a care in the world.

Heath made his living selling spells. Couldn't risk letting potential customers think he was afraid of someone else's magic. Be bad for business.

The lunchtime crowd bustled around Heath on the busy sidewalk. Most of them stuck in suits or business casual even in this heat, but scattered in among them were what Heath thought of as the Portlanders. The natives.

Some of the Portlanders were hipsters, of course, in baggy this or that and ironic tee shirts. Some had long hair, but even the ones who kept their hair short managed to get it in their eyes. Others were the flannel shirt crowd, in shorts instead of jeans, but the men kept thick beards even in this heat.

Fortunately many of the women wore sundresses, a sight for which Heath was always grateful.

Heath himself was dressed to almost blend in. Cream-colored cargo shorts with plenty of pockets for hiding a mojo bag or two, plus a number of little extras in case he needed them. Featherweight white, button-up shirt with short sleeves and no collar. Couple of breast pockets, though, for more of those extras.

Heath's black canvas backpack rested at his feet, against his suede boat shoes. Even when he wasn't under a death threat, Heath didn't go anywhere without that backpack and the arsenal he filled it with.

Heath wasn't thinking about spells just then though. He was just enjoying the sight of a young Japanese woman's shapely calves and reminding himself to call Nariko — his on-again-off-again girlfriend — and see how her trip to Japan was going. That was when someone interrupted his train of thought.

"You. You're the one they call Twilight, right?"

Heath sighed. He hated that nickname, and he hated that he hated it. Twilight was a magical time of day. Each dawn and dusk, a great time for conjuring or spelling or working with spirits. By all rights, Twilight should have been a great nickname for him.

But then those damned vampire books came out and ruined the whole thing. Heath knew a thing or two about vampires, and "romantic" was not a word he associated with them. "Dangerous," "deadly," and in most cases "ugly." Those were more the words he would have chosen.

Worst of all, some people — like Maggie's own grandmother — made the Twilight thing about Heath's skin tone. Not pale like his Irish mother, though he had her brown curls, but nowhere near as black as his father, though he had his daddy's dark brown eyes. Just somewhere in between, like so many things in Heath's life.

Heath took a long sip from his glass bottle of unsweetened iced tea before he turned to see who was asking.

Hipster kid. Baggy blue jeans, and a faded Madonna tour shirt that — if it were real — would be older than he was. Dishwater blond hair, just long enough to be in his eyes. Either a smooth shave or he didn't have to shave yet, though he held a paper bag like it had a can of beer in it. Probably Pabst Blue Ribbon or something.

Heath forced himself to smile. Kid could be a potential customer.

"Some people call me Twilight, yes. Something I can do for you?"

The kid pointed to the asphalt in the street. "They say you can read the future in the tar."

Heath looked where the kid was pointing, waited while a Prius chased an ancient LeMans up the street. Swirling black tar lines decorated the asphalt, leftover from some kind of street repair.

He looked back at the kid. "Yeah. Why?'

"I've been staring at that swirl for the last half-hour, trying to figure out what it means. What does it tell you?"

"Right now?" Heath looked again, as though considering it a serious question, then back at the kid. "Mostly that you don't know how divination works." Heath smirked as the kid flushed a bright red, but didn't leave him hanging. "Still, because there are people like me, you don't *have* to know how it works. If you have some money and a question you need an answer to, I could help you out."

"No need." The kid smiled, and it was a mean kind of smile. "I'll tell *your* future. Death will come for you on the third day, during the hour of Mars."

The kid turned and ran then. Shoelaces tied tight, which didn't fit the look. Unless, of course, the kid knew enough to be afraid, should Heath decide to punish the messenger for carrying a threat on his master's behalf.

Heath shook his head and sipped his tea, but his joy in the afternoon was gone. Drake had known Heath would make a public appearance. Had a response ready. Not good.

Heath felt as though he couldn't even quite taste the étouffée anymore. He thought about getting some beignets to try to recapture that moment, but someone behind him cleared their throat.

"Have I come at a bad time, Mr. Cyr?" A woman's voice, high and clear.

Heath stifled the sigh this time, and turned.

The woman standing in front of him practically had "money" stamped on her forehead.

It wasn't anything obvious. No jewelry except a simple gold circlet around her left wrist. No fancy watch, no designer purse. It was just … an air about her. Like a perfume. The way she carried herself, maybe.

Her lustrous blond hair hung just long enough to curl at her shoulders, without a single split end. Understated makeup, just enough to bring out the lighter shades of blue in her eyes. Pale green sheath dress that looked like breathable silk, cut just below the collar and just tight enough to leave no doubt that she kept her admirable body trim. Simple flats that matched the dress.

And even Heath's clever nose could barely pick up the honey-suckle of her actual perfume.

No, there was no one thing about this woman Heath could point to that made her look like she had money. But evaluating people was a big part of what Heath did, and he was certain this woman was loaded.

"That all depends," Heath said, "on why you've come."

"If you're in the middle of something..." She let the words hang. Her enunciation was letter perfect. Heath would have bet that if this woman said "bottle" he could hear both t's.

"Not at all," he said, with his best professional smile. "True, I did just finish my lunch break, and there are a few projects I really ought to get back to, but I could take a meeting right now, if it's convenient."

"Not here," she said, eyes darting back and forth among the crowd. "Could you accompany me to my office?"

"Certainly," said Heath. Something about this woman's speech or manner was bringing out the South in his manners. He'd have to watch that.

"Excellent." She gestured to a black Mercedes S-Class, pulling up to the curb. "Hershel will have us there in only a few minutes, and afterwards he can drop you wherever you like."

Yep. Definitely money.

———

THERE'S AN ART TO POLITE CONVERSATION THAT KEEPS MOVING, BUT never really says anything. And this woman was a past master of that art. She and Heath sat side-by-side in the rear, leather bucket seats of her black Mercedes, and though they talked the whole drive to her office, she didn't give away so much as her name, and she didn't ask Heath so much as the time.

Later Heath would try to remember just what they *did* talk about, but he was never quite sure. Maybe city history? Something about the bridges? But it didn't feel like tour-guide talk either.

It was just a non-discussion that continued as they crossed the

Willamette via the low Burnside Bridge, and all the way until they were parked in a reserved space in an underground lot beneath an eight-story office building. Heath wouldn't have been surprised to find the lot empty, but it looked busy as any parking lot on a weekday.

The moment the car was parked, the woman opened her own door and got out. Another surprise. Heath had expected the middle-aged Jewish guy, Hershel, to get out and open the doors. Escort them to the office. He had the big-guy-with-a-buzz-cut look of someone whose driving duties included personal protection. Probably had a Glock in a shoulder holster or something.

But Hershel sat in the car as though he expected to wait there for some time. Got out his phone and started playing a war game.

Heath shook his head and got out of the car. He started toward the closest elevator, set into the center of a broad, poured concrete pillar.

"Not that one," the woman said, pointing down along a clean red brick wall. "This way."

Tucked away behind another pillar was a second elevator. Dark green doors in the red brick, instead of that typical beige of parking lot elevators. Single button in its panel, but the woman didn't push it. Instead she ran her finger around its rim and whispered something.

Power. Heath felt a flicker of power when she did that. Seemed this woman was a practitioner after all, and one who had more than a little skill at hiding what she did. Normally Heath could spot another practitioner at fifty paces, but even now that he knew she had some skill, he could barely spot a flicker in the air about her.

"So that's how you knew to look for me," Heath said.

"Please," she said as the elevator door opened. "Wait until we're in the office."

The elevator had brown granite floor tiles that gleamed and brown wood-paneled walls. A button for each floor, but no posted permit, no special fire button, or any of the things Heath thought of as elevator safety measures.

"Not sure this is up to code," Heath said.

The woman only smiled and pushed the button for the eighth floor.

One office took up the whole eighth floor. The law firm of Benson and Benson. Antique-style desks, plush cream carpeting, phones with cords and the scent of old tobacco. This elevator dropped them off along a back wall near a row of closed-door offices that all had the word "partner" on their nameplates.

Heath could see clear across the open middle of the office, past the desks of paralegals and legal secretaries to where the other, public elevator let off on the other side of a glass door.

Here was the emptiness Heath was expecting. The other partners were all off today, it seemed, and had extended their largess to include their paralegals, legal secretaries, receptionists and others. Only the message lights flashing on the desk phones, the chilly air conditioning, and the motion-activated fluorescent tube lights in the acoustic ceiling above gave any hint that this was an active law firm.

"Boy," Heath said, "when you want privacy, you don't fool around."

Another smile, but no other answer. She led him along the row of partner offices. Six in all, each with a mahogany door and brass handle. Not knobs on these doors. Handles. A little latch at the top to be pushed down with the thumb, right under the key lock.

She stopped at the last office, as Heath knew she would. This one, unlike the others, was warded. She didn't try to hide how she opened it though. She just ran her finger down the lock as she whispered a little power at it, then opened the door as though it had never been locked in the first place.

More thick cream, spotless carpeting. More mahogany for the main desk and the bookshelves, which were filled with law books. Painting of a ship at sea in a storm alongside the requisite diplomas and Bar Association membership, but no photographs anywhere. High-end executive chair, royal blue, behind the big desk, currently facing a computer desk to one side, on which sat a great big honking monitor. No fluorescent bulbs in here. Old school yellow incandescent bulbs already burning in an elegant overhead lamp.

Oh, and huge, tinted windows overlooking the Willamette River.

She closed the door behind them before she took the big blue chair. Heath slipped his backpack off his shoulders and plopped himself on one of the two big, comfy, brown leather chairs set for clients, in front of the desk.

The smell of tobacco was stronger in here, even over the leather of Heath's chair. Strong enough that Heath could tell it was cigar tobacco, not cigarette or pipe.

"I presume you read the name on the door," she said.

"Yep." Heath shook his head. "But you're not Monica Benson."

"Perhaps you are less perceptive than I've been told, Mr. Cyr. Did you fail to notice—"

"The wards? Yeah, I saw them. Anti-scrying mostly, plus a couple of filigrees to keep out nosy spirits, I think?" Heath smiled. "Yes, they're your work. Have the same feel as that little breath of power you used to get us in here without tripping any of the alarms but without using a key, either."

"Ah, so you think I've led you in here illegally?" Confidence in that smile of hers, not conceit. Made her a little prettier, not that she needed the help.

"No. That'd be a stupid risk, and you don't strike me as the stupid type."

"So what *do* you think?"

"I think it's not every day another practitioner wants to hire me, so I'm curious about what exactly you want."

"You don't have any guesses?"

Heath smiled. "Sorry. *My* guesses have value, and you've gotten all I'm going to give you for free."

"That's fair," she said with a slight nod, then a small frown creased her forehead. "I suppose you'll need another name then."

"Nope." He shook his head and folded his hands across his stomach, wondering when she'd get to the point. "I give every one of my clients a personal nickname, just in case I need it." He smiled. "Works just as well as the name your momma gave you. At least, for my purposes."

Her sculpted eyebrows raised just a little.

"Is that a threat, Mr. Cyr?"

"It's nothing more than the answer to an implied question. Some clients don't want me to know their names because they think they can cheat me and I'll have no recourse." He shook his head. "Just not how the world works."

He let those words hang for a moment, but started up again before she could speak.

"Not saying that's why you don't want me to know your name. You have your own reasons, and your privacy is your business. I'm just saying, in my head, you're Goldilocks."

Goldilocks blinked, then smiled, then laughed, and it was nowhere near as smooth a sound as her cultivated speech. More like she was a street girl who made good.

"Goldilocks. I like that. I shall take it as a compliment."

Heath chose not to correct her. He smiled again, and said, "So, what can I do for you, Goldilocks?"

"I need you to kill a bear who thinks I've been sleeping in her bed."

Monica Benson's office was big, as offices go, but it wasn't big enough for the belly laugh Heath let out. Loud and long, both hands still folded across his stomach. Man, he hadn't laughed this hard since he hit that improv show with Colin last month.

Goldilocks didn't say anything through the whole gale of laughter. She didn't join in either. She just sat there with a long-suffering look in those blue eyes.

"I'm sorry," Heath managed at last. "It's just..." He had to chuckle a little more. "It's just, I mean, after all this clandestine crap. You bring me here, away from witnesses, behind your little anti-scry wards—"

"My wards are not—"

"I know, I know," Heath said, waving his hand. "Didn't mean to offend your work. They're good, fine wards. It's just that you were coming across as a smart woman, very together, with all your research done well ahead of time."

Laughter started bubbling out of him again. He clamped it down.

"But ... but I'm afraid you've mistaken me for my uncle. Understandable. We're both named Cyr. Mind you, he's more than a few years older, and he's got that Wesley Snipes dark skin, which I do not."

"I in no way mistook you for Andre Cyr." All business in those blue eyes now, and her tone was flat, like Heath had pissed her off. He wasn't sorry though. Might bring an earlier end to a meeting that was looking more and more like a waste of his time. She continued nonetheless. "If I wished to speak with Andre Cyr, I would have arranged a meeting when he was in town last month, or simply flown to New York to meet him there. I assure you, I know exactly to whom I am speaking."

To whom she is speaking. Apparently Goldilocks got formal when she was angry.

"Then you should have known in advance that you were wasting your time and mine. I do not commit murder. Not for love or money. You want to hire someone to do your killing for you, you might try the Lammergeyer. Italian fellow. Lives over in Vancouver."

"I know who the Lammergeyer is."

"Then you're better off asking him." Heath held up his hands. "Not saying he'd do it, mind you. Got no way of knowing that myself. Just strikes me as the type. Gives off a real *Cosa Nostra* vibe."

Goldilocks flared her nostrils in a slow sigh. "Have you quite finished with your merriment at my expense?"

"Not sure yet," Heath said with a shrug. "No way to know what you'll say next."

That got him a raised eyebrow. "Is this how you treat all your prospective clients?"

"Only the ones who ask me to commit murder."

"There's that phrase again, Mr. Cyr." She folded her hands in the center of the desk like she owned it. Almost like she really was this

Monica Benson. Maybe Goldilocks was an attorney after all. Make sense if she were, and Monica were a rival...

But Goldilocks was still talking.

"What it seems you do not understand is that murder is a *legal* distinction. For a killing to be murder, it must be accomplished by means that are provable in court beyond a reasonable doubt. Considering the percentage of the populace who believe that magic is fiction—"

"Just stop," Heath said, holding up a hand. "This isn't a college dorm, and this isn't some internet forum. I'm not interested in listening to you play games with definitions so you can try to make *murder* sound palatable."

"I'm not trying to make it sound palatable." She blinked in actual confusion, as though Heath had missed the point entirely. "I'm pointing out that I'm not asking you to commit murder. If I were, I'd be asking you to commit a crime. To risk jail time, and everything that comes with it. I would never ask that of you. I'm only asking you to take a life."

Heath had a rejoinder ready for that, but Goldilocks got louder.

"*Everyone dies, Mr. Cyr.* It's part of the definition of being human. Hastening the end of a life is no more wrong or unnatural than ending someone's cold or helping them find love, both of which have helped you achieve a level of notoriety in this city."

"So do it yourself."

"I have compelling reasons why I cannot, and they are not yours for the asking."

"Fair enough," Heath said. He crossed his feet up on the desk and regarded Goldilocks between the toes of his suede boat shoes. "Well I, too, have compelling reasons why I cannot. And I'll give you one for free — I don't kill for money."

"You may change your mind when you hear the name of the target."

"Not likely."

"Vizinha."

Heath started laughing again.

"Mr. Cyr," Goldilocks said in exasperated tones, "please. I assure you I'm quite serious."

"No," Heath said, getting his laughter under control. "You're not. You're either pranking me or you're stupid. Because if you know anything about the lay of the land in this town, you know that I tangled with Vizinha just last year and got my ass handed to me."

"I assure you, that is entirely my point. This is an opportunity for you to—"

Heath pulled his feet off the desk and sat forward in the big, comfy chair. He stabbed the desk with his finger as he interrupted her, just in case his own business tones weren't getting the point across.

"Now you listen here. It's only recently I've been able to come back from that beating, and only more recently still that she and I have buried the hatchet."

"Yes," Goldilocks said, leaning forward in her seat, excitement in those blue eyes now. "Exactly. When you two toasted each other at Gripper last week it was the talk of the town. Which makes this the perfect time. She won't be ready for you."

Heath sighed and rubbed the bridge of his nose before he tried one last time to explain.

"Look. Maybe among you ceremonial types, this is how things work. Me, I'm a root worker. A conjure man. I do Hoodoo and a little more besides, and I play along the edges of Vodou. Vizinha, she's what they call a *mãe-de-santo* in Quimbanda. Or maybe it's Umbanda. I've never been quite sure with her. Anyway, we don't exactly do the same kind of thing, but it's like we're ... spiritual cousins. Do you understand what I'm saying?"

Heath waited to continue until Goldilocks nodded. Took a moment, but she did, wariness all through her eyes.

"Vizinha and I understand each other in a way you and I never will. Even during our war, we didn't have to discuss terms, because they were just understood. There's a way things are done between people like us, and a way they're not. We know it. The spirits, they know it too. If one of us started playing fast and loose with the unwritten rules, we'd end up with more trouble than I think you understand."

Goldilocks furrowed her brow with a slight frown on those pouty lips. "So ... what I'm asking would violate pacts with the spirit world?"

Heath stifled a chuckle. No sense in insulting the woman when she was coming close to understanding.

"Not quite," he said. "But kind of like that. The point is, even if I were the sort of person who'd kill for money, I'd still have a bunch of other reasons to tell you no. And to be honest, I can think of a few good reasons to give Vizinha a call when we're done here."

Power flared around Goldilocks. Apparently she didn't like to hide herself when she felt threatened. Heath's fingers itched to pull a little ammunition from one of his pockets, but he held that urge in check.

"Mr. Cyr, I have trouble believing you would wish it known that you violated the sanctity of a client's privacy."

"There you go, calling yourself a client again when I've told you about a half-dozen times now that I'm not taking your job. I have no special love for Vizinha, but I have no special love for people who waste my time either."

Without taking her eyes from his, Goldilocks opened a desk drawer, took out a plain white envelope, and set it on the desk in front of him.

"For your time," she said.

Heath smiled. "Don't take this wrong, but why don't you just upend that envelope on the desk for me."

She matched his smile, but hers looked a little more serpentine. Still, she did as he asked. No symbols, sigils, runes, or odd little curlicues. No powder, oils or roots. Only crinkly old American cash. Two Franklins, a Hamilton, a Lincoln, and a couple of Washingtons. And not one of them showed so much as a hint of spell work. Two hundred seventeen dollars in clean cash.

"Sufficient for a consultation?" she asked in the confident tones of one who knew the answer.

"Yep," Heath said, scooping up the cash and slipping it into his shirt pocket. While his hand was in there, he palmed a small packet of a certain blend of powders. Just in case. "And since you're paying for it, here's your advice: steer clear of Vizinha. She's tough, she's smart, and she deals with the kind of spirits I personally like to forget exist. If she thinks you're banging someone she considers hers, either make it clear you're not or — if you are — stop right now and apologize."

"It's not that simple, Mr. Cyr."

"It never is. Except when that's how it's got to be." When that got him a puzzled look, Heath added, "Something my dad likes to say, and I think he's got the right of it."

"Well," Goldilocks said, in the deep-breathed style of someone coming to a conclusion, "if I cannot hire you to do the deed, I suppose I cannot hire you to consult with me while I — how did you put it? — *tangle* with her?"

The word *no* almost made it past Heath's lips, but he chewed on it a moment as he thought. Going up against Vizinha himself was one thing. Advising someone else, though...

"As long as you pay cash in advance for every consultation, same fee you just gave me, I'll be happy to point out your mistakes for you."

"I'll require you to meet with me at dawn, every Tuesday, Friday and Saturday until this matter is resolved."

Heath couldn't have heard that right. "At *dawn*?"

"Hershel shall pick you up fifteen minutes before the sun rises, and we shall meet here for thirty minutes each time, to discuss strategy."

Heath worked his mouth around while he thought about that. On the one hand, this woman wanted her meetings at dawn. Great time for certain kinds of workings, but not a time Heath's eyes were open if he could help it.

On the other hand, six hundred fifty-one dollars a week for just under two hours work, including travel time. Might get as much as two weeks pay before Goldilocks got beat too badly to continue.

"Got yourself a deal," he said.

"Hershel will see you home then," she said. "I trust you can show yourself out? There's more I must do before I leave."

Something about the way she said that. Maybe it was her choice of words, maybe it was her tone, or maybe it was the distance in those blue eyes. Or maybe it was just that she didn't offer to shake hands to seal the agreement. Whatever it was made the hairs on the back of Heath's neck stand up, and little hints of discomfort crawl up his back.

As Heath made his quick way out of the office, he began to suspect he'd undercharged for this job. Even if it *was* just a consultancy.

2

"YOU UNDERCHARGED AGAIN."

Nariko had the kind of willowy beauty and long, glittering black hair that made American Japanophiles fall to their knees — sometimes literally — but her expression as she said those words was as ugly as her tone. Probably didn't help that her expressive jade-green eyes were hidden behind sunglasses. Which was weird, because it had to be close to midnight where she was.

And it definitely didn't help that she spoke loudly into the phone as she and Heath had their daily video chat.

As far as Heath could tell, she was on a subway of some kind, and she was packed in tight among the citizens of Yokohama, at least a third of whom were also on the phone and speaking in loud, fast Japanese.

A little irritating that this was where she was for their call. Yes, she was in Japan "visiting relatives," which was the part she would admit to of a trip that Heath suspected of being something much bigger. Something she didn't want to tell him about because she didn't want to worry him.

Nariko held back a lot on family matters. Heath's own family was messed up enough that he tried to give her plenty of space on that front, but he couldn't help feeling frustrated that she cut him out that way.

No doubt whatever she was doing kept her busy, and maybe kept her from planning much about her days. But still, just once it would have been nice if she'd found someplace quiet and private for their talk.

Heath, for his part, always made sure he was home when it was time to call.

Home was a backyard apartment in Northwest Portland, near gigantic Forest Park. Heath lived there rent-and-utility-free, thanks to a little misadventure on behalf of his landlord. Hadn't provided the outcome the landlord wanted, but that wasn't Heath's fault, and the man was smart enough to hold up his end of the deal.

Heath sat on his front porch in one of the two matching white plastic chairs — the kind that were designed to mimic their wooden cousins — surrounded by the native plants of the backyard: Corsican mint for ground cover, ferns, roses, rhododendrons, Oregon grapes, and a half-dozen tall, mighty Douglas fir trees.

Nariko was yelling her words at Heath from a subway car. Heath was practically sitting in a forest, complete with birdsong and chittering squirrels.

And the birds and the squirrels were on his side, Heath was certain. Not that telling her that would do any good.

The sounds and smells of summer air and nature helped Heath keep hold of his temper as Nariko continued.

"I don't know how many times I have to tell you. *Value your work. Value your time.* And in this case, value your risks. How is Vizinha going to take it when she finds out you're acting as war counselor for her enemy?"

"Do I get to talk now?" Heath said.

"I don't know," Nariko said. "Are you going to say something stupid?"

"I do love our little chats, Nari. But I've obviously caught you at the wrong time, so—"

"No, no, Heath. Tell me what you've got to say. Because I won't forgive you if you get yourself killed while I'm out of the country."

"Well, you know I can't promise that. Not any more than you can promise not to get killed while you're doing ... whatever it is you're about over there that you aren't sharing with me."

Nariko's face went blank so fast it was like someone switched her off.

"Yeah," Heath said. "You like to tell me I'm dumb in all the wrong ways, but no one does what I do for a living without understanding *when* one plus one equals three."

"We were talking about you and your recent business mistake." All the anger was gone from her voice now. She sounded ... guarded. And that hurt enough to twist Heath's stomach.

"Yeah," Heath said with a sigh, settling back into his chair and wondering just how long Colin would need to find the beers in Heath's fridge. A drink just sounded entirely too good. "By all means, let's stick to my problems so you can feel righteous."

"Heath, I—"

"No, no, you asked a question and I haven't answered it." Heath's heart was pounding now, and he had to work to keep his tone even, so he worked a little harder to push it past even to light. As though everything was just as fine as Nariko wanted to pretend it was on her end. "You wanted to know how Vizinha would respond? Well I'll tell you. She'd laugh, and ask me how much I got out of Goldilocks for the effort."

Nariko's mouth pursed. Heath couldn't see her eyes, but he was betting he'd have seen confusion in them, if he could.

"Yeah, I know. Not how you'd react. But she doesn't think like you, Nari. Doesn't think like me either, but she comes closer." Heath pursed his lips, then said, "Look at it this way. Say you're coaching a football team, and you find out the other side has hired as a consultant the guy who lost to you in last year's big game. Are you going to be afraid of what he has to say?"

"No," Nariko said, sounding more relaxed and at least a little abashed. "Because that consultant doesn't know how to beat you." Her lips quirked in a little smirk. A hopeful sign, but it vanished quickly. "Vizinha will see this as you undermining her enemy's confidence, won't she? Doing her a favor and getting paid for it."

"Now you're coming closer. In that sense, it's a win-win."

"True." Nariko nodded. "But Heath, it's never going to go that simply and you know it."

Heath tried to interject, but Nariko was building up steam again.

"You don't know anything about this Goldilocks or what her reasons are. You don't even know what her plan really is, except that it might, *might* involve killing Vizinha. And you've agreed to consult with her anyway."

"For—"

"For entirely too little money, all things considered."

"Hey, the amount—"

"Was exactly what she offered you for hush-money level consultation services. For a wartime consultation, you could have doubled that for each meeting and she'd have paid it. Hell, if you'd show half as much interest in negotiation as you do in grinding your herbs, you could have gotten triple."

"Nari, I—"

"Never listen to anything I say about business?" She sighed. "No. I know. You are beautiful, Heath. So beautiful it hurts sometimes. And you have a good heart, despite everything you've been through. But—"

"Let me guess. I'm dumb in all the wrong ways?"

That got the first smile out of Nariko he'd seen on the call. Then some suited jackass ruined it by bumping into her. She slammed an elbow into the guy's back, knocking him forward.

Heath could see him turn to say something. Nariko turned away from the phone's camera, her mouth tightening into a line as she did.

The guy held up surrendering hands, bowed from the neck up, and backed away.

Heath didn't blame him. Her hair was down, but she was dressed for business. Black leather biker jacket, high-cut tight mauve shirt. If she'd had her hair up, Heath would have demanded to know just how much trouble she was in.

As it was, he knew just what expression she must have had when she faced that guy, and Heath was sure it promised violence. One of the ways Nariko had kept the Japanophiles at bay here in Portland was by establishing a resting bitch face that could melt steel. And that was without trying. When she *tried*...

Just thinking about it, Heath shuddered.

She turned back to the camera. "My stop's coming up. I better go. Tell you what, I'll give you a wake-up call tomorrow from someplace quiet. Maybe we can talk without getting at each other's throats."

"It's a lovely thought," Heath said. "Shame you're so far away. We're always at our best when whatever we're doing can be followed by getting naked."

"Well," Nariko said with a sly smile, "be a good boy and promise not to get yourself killed, and maybe I'll give you a wake-up treat."

"I can promise to try," Heath said.

"He'll be good," Colin said, quickly coming through the white front door behind Heath, which meant Nariko could see him as well as hear him. "I'll see to it myself."

"Thank you, Colin," Nariko called, then blew Heath a kiss and disconnected.

"Dude," Colin said, closing the door behind him and handing Heath a sweating bottle of Deschutes Hefeweizen, "she's offering you *video* phone sex and you can't make a promise? What is *wrong* with you?"

Colin dropped onto the other plastic chair, which somehow creaked in protest even under his skinny ass. Colin was dressed for the summer afternoon heat: camo cargo shorts, Birkenstocks, and a Halestorm tee shirt with the sleeves ripped off. Smelled a bit of sunscreen, which was a change from his usual scent of baked goods, but not a shock. He had the kind of white skin that might burn under a full moon, and his long blond hair was so fine it didn't offer his scalp or neck all that much protection.

On the other hand, a black tee shirt, even with the sleeves ripped off, would never be as cool as Heath's plain white, button-up, collarless shirt. And Heath was glad his own cargo shorts were cream-colored. His matching clothes with Colin would never have sat well with either of them.

As Colin took his first sip of the Hef, Heath said, "'bout time you got back with the beers."

"Hey, I knew how Nariko would take the news of your latest job and death threat. No need for me to listen in on *that*." He held up the beer in toast. "But stand by and let you pass up a dirty video call? I couldn't do that and still call myself your friend."

Heath clinked the beers, then said, "I didn't tell her about the death threat."

Heath took a long swig of the crisp Hef, while Colin's blue-gray eyes got so wide they could have swallowed his beer bottle.

"She. Will. Kill. You." Colin shook his head. "Figuratively, I mean. Assuming you don't get literally killed." He swallowed, then blinked. "Then she'd kill me. And maybe literally, in that case."

Heath chuckled. "She has no right to bitch. I called her out on the fact that she's doing something big and dangerous over there, and she still wouldn't tell me what."

"I'm sorry, did you just attempt to apply logic to an emotional situation?" Colin snorted. "If Drake manages to put you in the ground before Nariko gets back, she will kill him. She may not even bother with magic to do it. Then, the next morning, I'll wake up with the tip of that steel hair spike of hers hovering just below my nostril."

"You have spirits and wards to keep that from happening."

"So does Mandrake. So do you. Think they'd keep Nariko out when she's up for vengeance?"

Heath took a swig of his beer. No point in answering that. But then something else occurred to him.

"That's why you came over, isn't it? To check on my defenses and lend me a hand if I need it."

"Nariko scares me," Colin said with a shrug. "Mandrake doesn't."

A horn sounded. Not a car horn, or a semi's horn, or even a train horn. Heck, even far away as the Willamette river was from Heath's place, a boat horn would have sounded more at home than this noise.

This horn sounded like something out of a *Lord of the Rings* movie. The kind of thing ... an old army ... would use...

Something was at the border of Heath's outer wards.

THE BIRDS AND THE SQUIRRELS SHUT UP.

Never a good sign, when the birds and squirrels got quiet in the middle of a summer afternoon, especially in the yard at Heath's place. One minute, they'd been going on about ... whatever squirrels and birds went on about — Heath didn't *quite* understand them, not the way he understood frogs and crickets — and the next they were still as if they'd all just turned to stone.

Even Colin noticed.

"Well, *that's* creepy," he said.

"Creepier than the ... what ... hunting horn I guess it was?"

Colin turned and looked Heath squarely in the eye. "You heard a hunting horn?"

"You didn't hear it?"

They were both quiet for a long moment. Heath heard a high-revving motorcycle speed by in the background, a helicopter whuf-whuffing nearby, and maybe a street away someone was mowing their lawn. No second blast yet, but the implications of that horn soured the crisp taste of the beer on Heath's tongue.

"Breeze has stopped," Colin said. "But I don't hear any horn."

The birds took off. Maybe twenty or so had been in the trees in the yard, but at some hidden signal they all took wing at the same time.

"What was this horn?" Colin asked. "Tell me exactly what it sounded like."

"Like something out of a *Lord of the Rings* movie."

"The horn of Gondor or the horn of Rohan?"

Heath didn't flatter that with a response. He did not share Colin's geekier tastes and Colin knew it. Instead Heath got out of his chair, took a sip of beer to freshen the taste in his mouth, stepped out onto a patch of smooth brown dirt, and spat straight up.

The spittle fell to his right. A moment later, confirmation came from off that direction. The horn sounded again. *Horrr-oooo, horr-oooo.*

Heath wasn't sure how he reacted to that, but he must have done something. Colin sat up straight. Cleared his throat. "You heard it again, didn't you?"

Heath nodded.

"Not a good sign that you can hear it and I don't."

Heath agreed, but didn't see any point in stating the obvious.

"I've got a spirit that's pretty good at recon. Want me to have him check it out?"

Heath shook his head, still staring off to the right. All he could see was the row of twelve-foot-tall arborvitae that served as a fence between this yard and the neighbor. The neighbor's golden retriever was quiet, but she'd been quiet all afternoon. Probably take your dog to work day.

"You sure?" Colin asked, and Heath could hear the nerves in his friend's voice. He wanted to help.

"Save it," Heath said. "Don't need recon to know these are probably legionnaires working for whatever demon Drake summoned, coming to have the groundhog shake my hand. Doesn't mean they'll get past my confusion ward."

"Confusion ward?"

"Not the first time someone's come after me, and my general philosophy is 'they can't kill me if they can't find me.' So I've laid a few tricks to make finding my home just a little bit harder for anybody out to do me harm."

"So that's why Nariko's ex- never showed up to kick your ass, like he threatened?"

"Maybe," Heath said with a shrug, much more of his attention looking for the little signs that would tell him how the demons were doing against his wards. "More likely Nariko had a talk with him."

The horn sounded again, from somewhere to the rear now, and

Heath turned to follow the *horr-oooo, horr-oooo*. The back fence of the property was redwood crawling with red and pink roses. Not arborvitae like the side fences, because the neighbor to the rear had a Great Dane. And that Great Dane started barking and running toward the front of his owner's property, pissed as all hell that something so unnatural dared come close to *his* people.

The demons weren't that close, of course. That was part of the spell. Triggering a little deception for the six-year-old puppy, in case something like this happened when Heath was sleeping and he needed to wake up. The booming bark of that Great Dane was more than enough to rouse him from even a deep sleep.

Maybe not the kindest thing to do to that poor dog, though, so Heath had treats delivered anonymously every so often. A big rawhide bone, the last time. The kind of thing that might puzzle the owner, but would always end up with the pup. And Heath blessed every one of those presents himself, before he had them delivered, to help make sure the Great Dane lived a long and happy life.

Least he could do.

Anyway, it looked as though the demons were following the false trail well enough. That should lead them back away for now, and if they'd passed the point of triggering the Great Dane...

Heath counted to twenty Mississippi, nice and slow, holding up a hand to silence Colin when he started to ask a question. Colin chanted some kind of spell instead, something that sounded like words in an old language — Latin or Hebrew maybe — but still didn't sound quite right to Heath.

When Heath reached twenty Mississippi, he stepped up to his front door, set his beer down inside it, and closed it. He took a moment to regard the black, hand-painted, equal armed cross and old fashioned key in the center of the white door, his little tributes to Papa Legba at the entrance to his home.

Heath kissed the first two fingers of his right hand, then touched the center of the cross and the teeth of the key. "Please, Papa," he said, "keep an eye on this little fool's home while he's away."

In a quick, practiced move, Heath whipped out his keys, locked the door, and slipped them right back into his pocket.

"What's going on?" Colin asked, as Heath grabbed his black canvas backpack from the porch beside his chair and slung it over one shoulder.

"Did you drive?"

"Yes," Colin said, immediately downing his beer rather than leave it unfinished. Didn't matter. Alcohol never seemed to have any effect on Colin beyond getting him a little red-faced, any more than overeating did anything worse than make him pat his belly. Heath didn't know what New Age, self-help magic book had given Colin the secret to keeping his body on the healthy side of skinny, but it definitely worked for him.

But then, those books were every bit as reliable for Colin as roots and powders were for Heath. Didn't matter how silly or over-the-top the sales language and "testimonials" got in those old 70s books like *Voltarr Power* and *The Unbeatable Magic Tome of Frater Kalam*. In Colin's hands, they were good as gold.

"Good," Heath said. "We're taking your car then."

He started across the flat stepping stone pathway through the dirt between plants and Corsican mint ground cover, heading for the redwood gate that led to the driveway and the street beyond.

"Hey!" Colin said, hurrying to catch up with Heath's long strides. "Where are we going?"

"I thought it was obvious," Heath said with a smile. "We're hunting demons."

THE PASSENGER SEAT OF COLIN'S LITTLE WHITE SATURN SEDAN WAS pretty cramped, and the whole car smelled like French fry grease. Not the place Heath would have chosen to go rummaging through his backpack, but better than trying to do that while driving. And the car's interior was pleasantly neutral in terms of colors — gray cloth for the seats and carpet, black plastic molding for everything else — and spells, in that there were none.

Heath still had trouble believing that. Nariko's motorcycle was heavily enchanted, and Heath wouldn't even get behind the wheel of a car that didn't at least have a good strong *ignore-me-mr.-policeman* charm on it.

But then, Colin was a white boy. Probably never needed a charm like that.

"Um," Colin said, starting the car, "exactly where will we be hunting demons? Oh, yeah, and *why*?"

"Where is going to be up Cornell, over by Macleay Park. Know it?"

"Yeah. Up the hills, right?"

"Right," Heath said, pulling out a purple skull candle and dusting it off with a pure white handkerchief as he examined the carvings. Everything looked good, and Heath could still smell the cedar, ginseng and licorice root he'd worked into the wax as he made it.

Hand-blended wax of his own concoction, and hand-carved into the shape of a human skull. And a pretty darn good likeness if he said so himself.

He'd made this candle to trap a demon. A legionnaire in the service of a reputed marquis of Hell: Samigina. Never did get to use it, because it turned out not to be a legionnaire after that boy, but Samigina himself. Or herself, maybe. Heath hadn't been too clear on that point, but then, demons weren't really his brand of bourbon.

Either way, that candle would never have been strong enough to contain a marquis. Only wits and willpower got Heath out of that one.

Appropriate, that the candle would be used to trap a demon sent by Drake. That Samigina business was what put Heath at odds with Drake in the first place. He was the one who's sent the demon after the boy. And he'd been none too pleased when he found out how Heath had interfered, even though Heath's interest had been purely professional.

He'd been well-paid to get the demon off that kid's back. The first real step in recovering Heath's reputation after the Vizinha disaster.

Meanwhile, Colin was steering his little car through the narrow streets of Northwest Portland, winding his way up the heavily forested west hills. Trees and ferns everywhere, and plenty of black-berry brambles. Just another reminder to Heath that, unlike Manhattan where he grew up, Portland felt more like a forest than a city. Wilder, and more untamed. As though houses and buildings just happened to grow in copses and groves alongside all these Douglas firs.

More traffic on the way up the hills than Heath would have liked.

It was late enough in the day now that there might not have been as many tourists on their way up to the Pittock Mansion, but commuters were making their way home, and those who'd already been home were out on their bikes, slowing everything down.

Heath had the misfortune of being anti-bicycle in a very pro-bicycle city. Far as Heath was concerned, if people wanted to ride their bikes for exercise, they could take them on the countless trails around town, or, even better, in the surrounding suburbs. For trans-portation, they either needed to walk, or to join the twenty-first century and use a motor, as God intended.

Heath didn't have time for bicyclists today though, not even the arrogant bastard in lime green spandex who flipped off Colin for passing him.

Instead, Heath opened his spirit eyes and double-checked every-thing about the candle. Looked just as good as the day he made it, which also told him the preservation charms he put on his backpack were still good for at least another week.

"Wicked," Colin said. "Really. Look good in Eddie's hands on an Iron Maiden album cover. But you still haven't told me *why* we're out hunting demons instead of staying on your front porch, drinking beer in perfect safety."

"You've never really squared off with anyone, have you?"

"I don't have your gift for making enemies." Colin tapped his horn at the four-by-four that apparently intended to proceed up the hill at the blistering pace of fifteen miles per hour. "Come on, guy. If my little engine can make it to twenty-five at this angle, so can yours."

"Well, think. What's the most valuable asset in a spell war?"

"A good knockout punch?"

"Information." Heath held up the candle. "Anything I trap in here will shift its loyalty to me, instead of Drake. And that should be good for all kinds of information."

"You know there might be more than one demon we're following, right? I mean, it *has* occurred to you that one person, hunting alone, doesn't need a horn?"

"Of course." Heath tucked the skull candle back into his backpack, then shook the backpack so the contents rattled. "Why do you think I carry the rest of this?"

Colin took an abrupt right turn onto a side street and parked under an oak tree, behind a big blue pickup truck. He turned a serious expression to Heath, who was none too happy about the sudden detour. He stared back at Colin, breathing slowly through his nose and trying to unclench his jaw.

Getting angry at Colin wouldn't help. Though what Colin said next sorely tested that theory.

"This is stupid. What can this demon tell you that your cards and cowries can't? You're better at divination than anyone I know, this side of the Sybil. Better, in the sense that you don't answer questions with riddles. And I *know* you've got spirits for recon, same as I do, and between us we can find out plenty. So what's the real deal? Why do this?"

Heath clucked his tongue, then flared his nostrils in a deep breath. He puffed it out slowly while looking out the window, trying to set aside his irritation by marveling that anyone would set up a basketball hoop on a street with at least an eighteen-degree slope, and that wasn't counting the rest of the hill. One bad miss and that ball was *gone*...

There. That was enough. Heath turned back to Colin, who was looking more nervous now. Maybe re-thinking the wisdom of his words.

Heath held up a hand to reassure him.

"Two things." He held up his index finger. "One, the information I'd get from divination is different than I'd get from the demon, if only because of Drake's own wards." He held up a second finger. "Two, I deplete my enemy's resources, even just a little, while increasing my own. It's just good strategy."

"It's a risk, Heath. For all you know, this is a trap to lure you out of your wards."

"The entire war with Vizinha I never left the house. Drake and Vizinha were pretty chummy, just last month. If he was quizzing her about my tactics and defenses, he has no reason to expect me to do this."

"Doesn't make it a smart idea." Colin shook his head. "I still say it's a risk you don't need to take."

Heath's right hand itched with the desire to slap some sense into Colin, but Heath chose another slow, deep breath instead.

"Colin, if you don't start driving, I'm going to get out of the car and walk the rest of the way." Heath sighed. "This is happening. You can help or you can go home."

Colin sighed through his nose. "All right, but remember — I'm only half-kidding about Nariko. She might really murder me if I let you get killed."

That was so absurd that Heath couldn't help smiling. Even felt a little chuckle bubble at the back of his throat.

"So," he said, "what you're telling me is that you don't think Nariko knows how stubborn I can be? That she really believes you can talk me out of doing whatever the hell I decide I need to do?"

Colin started snickering like a cartoon dog, and that was it. Heath was laughing now.

"Fine!" Colin said, starting the car and pulling a u-turn in the middle of the block. "But you better get hold of that laughter. Maybe you don't think you'll need your A-game for this, but I do."

Heath tried to stop laughing all at once, but it didn't help. He had a nonstop chuckle going.

Suddenly Heath was glad about all that traffic. Gave him time to pull himself together before they got to the spot.

And as they made their slow way, Heath uttered a silent prayer. *Papa Legba, please keep an eye on us little fools today. I think we'll need it.*

"THERE!" HEATH SAID. "PULL OVER THERE."

He was pointing at a turnout that almost seemed to pop out of nowhere as they came around a bend to the right. Colin jerked the wheel immediately and then they were kicking up dust on the side of the road.

As turnouts went, it wasn't much. Scarcely two dozen feet between the paved road and the fir-and-blackberry-lined border of Macleay Park. Macleay Park was a subsection of immense Forest Park, as far as Heath could tell. Enough trees and undergrowth to discourage anyone who thought this might be a great place to leave their car while taking a hike. As if the hundred-foot descent down an almost vertical slope wouldn't have done the trick.

The sun was hidden behind the trees where they stood, and the air was dry and dusty, flavored with the scent of the fir trees and the unmistakable smell of cars.

"Kind of a busy spot," Colin said, referring to the line of traffic continuing up the hill. They were moving almost thirty now, which must have felt like seventy-five, slow as the first part of the ascent had been.

"Can't be helped," Heath said, picking a spot for his candle. Once the candle was in place he drizzled red, powdered chalk out of his hand to enclose the skull candle in a triangle that measured four feet on a side.

"Thought you didn't believe in the Triangle of Art."

"I don't." Heath clapped the dust off his hands. "But demons tend to like them, or so I hear."

"That *is* what it says in the books," Colin conceded.

Heath dug into his backpack for the bedpan, his mini saucepan incense censer. He gave it a shake to settle the salt at the bottom, then fished out the fresh piece of charcoal from under the salt. He lit it with a match from his Dollar Store pack and tossed the spent match over his shoulder.

Colin *tsked* at him, then picked up the match and put it in the trash bag he kept in the door of his Saturn.

Next Heath took out the symbol and sigil covered three-inch-by-three-inch cherry wood box that housed travel packs of his own blended incenses. In this case, he selected a packet mixture of acacia, dandelion and mugwort. Good for summonings and callings.

"Heath," Colin said. "I can feel them nearby. Can't you?"

"Yes," Heath said. And it was true. He could. After a fashion, anyway.

Time was, he wouldn't have recognized the way the hair stood up on his arms and the back of his neck as signs that there were demons nearby, but sad to say that time was past. He'd been around too many now. And he knew *that* was true when he'd realized he'd started differentiating demons from other spirits.

Had it really only been these last few months? How the time flew.

Horrr-oooo, horr-oooo.

"Heath?" Colin asked, a tremble through his voice. "That's more like the horn an Uruk-hai would blow."

"You can hear it now?" Heath didn't look up as he continued setting up. He did snap his fingers though. "That's right, you cast another spell, didn't you?"

"Yeah. And I'm getting report from one of my watchers. There are two dozen angry spirits roaming around, hunting you. And they're all circling around..."

"The next turnout," Heath said, "maybe a hundred yards down the road."

Heath gave Colin a smile, but Colin was blinking in confusion, as though a half-dozen questions tried to make it out of his mouth at the same time, and got bottlenecked somewhere behind his eyes.

"'s why I chose the place," Heath said, pausing for a small prayer as he knelt just outside the triangle and lit the coal, then put his incense box away. "I anchored the endpoint of my little runaround charm at the next turnout. Only place on the whole hillside where there are two turnouts this close together. Must be driving them crazy that they can sense me there, but can't find anything to sink their weapons into."

"Until they notice you're right ... here?"

Heath was smiling and patting his left boat shoe, where he'd tucked away something he'd never actually show anyone.

"Gotta feed this conjure hand a little extra this week. Doing *such* a good job."

Colin smiled and shook his head. "What can I do?"

"Two things." Heath paused with a pinch of incense held over the burning charcoal. "One, keep the drivers from noticing anything odd going on. Wouldn't do to have someone interfere at the wrong time. Two, on the off-chance I manage to pull more than one, be ready to help."

"On it," Colin said, and started to turn, but then turned back. "Wait. Before you get started, maybe tell me how this is going to work?"

Heath sighed and pulled back the hand holding incense pinched between his index finger and thumb.

"Demons focus better than humans, as a rule, but not too much better than any other spirit. And with these guys hunting hard for me, they've got to cast their awareness here and there or they'll never find me. So, all I do is start calling. Nice and soft and quiet. Too quiet, at first, for them to hear. But I slowly let it get a little louder and a little louder yet."

Colin drew breath with a smile on his face, and Heath cut him off.

"If you make a reference to the song 'Shout' I will send any demons I trap after you."

Colin held up his hands in surrender.

"Shouldn't be too long before one notices the call and comes to check it out. I stop calling then, and that should keep the others off my back while I *snatch* the investigator. And then we're out of here before the rest of the hunters are any the wiser. Just one more fox escaping the hounds."

"That ... sounds like it might actually work."

"Your confidence is overwhelming."

Colin shrugged again, and Heath gave him a moment to do his thing. Apparently his thing required him to pull a laminated magic square out of a pocket in his cargo shorts and rattle off some words that sounded more like backwards English than Latin.

But then, Heath wasn't exactly an expert in Latin.

Quick flare of power, and that was it. Colin turned around then, so whatever he did must have finished. That was fine, though. Heath trusted him to do his part right.

Heath scattered his pinch of incense on the coal, and the pungent mugwort was first smell to hit his nostrils, making him think of swamps and damp places.

"Hey, lookee here," whispered Heath in proper compelling tones. Any conjure man worth his roots knew all the little tricks of compulsion, and when the eyes weren't available because he couldn't see the target, the voice was the next best thing. "Something interesting over here. Something you ought to check out. May be nothing. But it may just be something big. Bigger even than your target. Come look. Come see for yourself. Come check it out."

Only a trickle of compulsion over those whispered words. A tiny drizzle of honey over the sugar cubes. He leaned forward on his knees, ignoring the way the rocky dirt ground into his skin. He held his focus on the thread of smoke from his incense and the words he whispered into it.

Invitations. Suggestions. Nothing strong. Nothing truly compelling. And nothing that would overpower the trick he'd laid at the next turnout, so not enough to bring the whole pack of demons down on his head.

"Come on, now," he cajoled. "I know you want to come see this. You can feel it, can't you? Such a big deal. Maybe. Maybe not. Never know until you come check it out for yourself. Better do it fast, before someone else notices. Then you won't get the credit. Someone else will, and you'll feel dumb then, won't you? Come on, now. Come see. Come see..."

And right in the middle of Heath's litany, the whole pack of demons descended on him.

3

THE BEST PART ABOUT HAVING A PACK OF DEMONS DESCENDING ON Heath — if, indeed, there was anything good about it — was that his spirit eyes were closed.

There were some types of spirits Heath wanted to see, and there were other types he *needed* to see, and there were times he didn't have much choice about the matter either way.

But demons, those Heath always hated to look at. They were never quite any one thing, always with the head of this and the body of that, and maybe the legs of something entirely different. Not to mention the wings some insisted on having. And half of them leered, while the other half looked at him like he was something they'd found fermenting for a week in a Dumpster.

So when it all went down, Heath did enjoy a fleeting thought that at least his spirit eyes were closed.

One moment Heath had just been kneeling outside his red chalk triangle, in that little dirt turnout some halfway up the hills of West Portland, with a drop-off into Forest Park on his right and heavy traffic on the city street to his left. Whispering sweet nothings into the purple-brown smoke of his smelly incense, trying to call just loud enough to pull a single straggler from the demons hunting him.

The next, well...

Every hair south of his scalp stood up all at once, and the western meadowlarks that Heath hadn't realized he could hear all stopped singing. His stomach gave that little pucker it always did when something bad was coming in fast.

He looked up and saw a baker's dozen of ripples in the air. Heat waves that didn't quite look like muscled human bodies carrying spears. Worst of all, even with his spirit eyes closed, he could sort of see the leader.

That wasn't good. His whole life Heath had gotten a good look at maybe two dozen spirits when his spirit eyes were closed, and none of them were things he wanted to see. Up until that day, the worst had been that weird, six-limbed *thing* that guarded Uncle Andre twenty-four-seven and could even slip past some pretty impressive wards.

But this demon, this was worse.

Through that blurriness like heat waves, Heath could see a red humanoid with fur the color of nasty bruises. Its body was twice as thick as a man's ought to be, and not an ounce of it looked like fat. Had the head of a jackal, black as onyx, and orange eyes that sparked and sparkled with malicious glee. Its high, tall ears were pierced six times each, and had barbed, steely rings looping through them.

It carried a maul that made John Henry's hammer look like a child's toy.

The first spear came winging through the air at Heath, but missed by the span of a fly's wing. Just more proof that even demons weren't unbeatable. They'd been tricked here by Heath's conjuring, and that spear missed because of the mojo in Heath's pocket.

But his mojo could do only so much, and there were an awful lot of demons. And it probably wouldn't do anything at all against that maul.

"Heath," Colin said, a tremor all through his voice. Poor bastard probably had that spell still going and was getting an eyeful of the kind of misery Hell had to offer.

If they really came from Hell. Heath wasn't too clear on that point.

"Slow 'em down," Heath said, trying for all the confidence he could muster. "I'll do the rest."

"Why bother?" said the leader. It had a voice like a steam whistle: high, loud, and annoying.

It raised a clawed hand, and all twelve of its lackeys raised spears. Including the one who'd already thrown. That just wasn't fair.

Of course, it wasn't as though they were throwing physical spears...

"You have no need to interfere, Colin Amadeus Driscoll," the big furry demon said. "We have not been sent for you, and tasty as I might find you, while on a mission we will not kill or harm any who do not obstruct us."

"All that it takes for evil to triumph," Colin said, "is for good men to do nothing."

That made the demon turn to look at Colin. "And *you* call yourself a *good* man?"

"I'm here," Colin said with a shrug. "And Heath is my friend. That's close enough for me."

"Very well," the demon said. "We get to kill you too."

"Wait!" Heath held up a hand, thinking just as fast as he could.

A straight-up fight was the last thing he wanted. In fact, a straight-up fight was just about the last thing Heath ever wanted. He much preferred the sucker punch, the unexpected strike. As far as Heath was concerned, a fight ought to consist of nothing more than a single blow, struck when his opponent was asleep, or maybe caught up in something else...

...maybe that was why he lost to Vizinha.

Heath shook his head, getting back on track while the demon leader cackled a sound that grated along every nerve in Heath's body.

"Don't tell me," the demon said with a leer. Always the leer with these guys. "You wish to challenge me to single combat, to save your friend and take the noble death instead of suffering simple slaughter at the hands of me and my fellows?"

"Close enough," said Heath, rubbing his chin, "though I must say I do see a bit of a sticking point."

"And what, pray tell, is that?"

Curiosity. Heath was sure he heard actual curiosity in the demon's screaming-high voice. Heath's improvised plan might just work out after all.

"Well, I'm a pretty straight shooter, and known as such. When I make a bargain with a spirit or a client, you can believe I'm going to move heaven and earth to keep it." Heath shook his head. "But you and yours aren't exactly known for keeping your side of..."

"I have been constrained to find and kill you." The demon waved that huge-ass maul to indicate the dozen spears trained on Heath. "As you can see, I'm keeping a bargain right now. What's more, within the parameters of that arrangement, I have a certain amount of ... leeway to deal."

The demon's leer widened. "And I must say, the chance to kill you myself while these others stand by, only getting to watch, fills me with pleasure."

"Good, but—"

"And understand, your death will not come quickly. Oh no. If I bargain with you and win, I may take my time with you. Your death will be slow and sweet. You will know such pain that the worst agony you've ever experienced will seem blissful repose by comparison."

Heath swallowed, glad for the sweat breaking out on his brow and the flutter in his stomach and knees. Oh, he was every bit as scared as he looked, but functioning while frightened had been part of his life since his uncle tried to bury him alive as an offering to Baron Samedi.

And right now, he needed to *look* frightened. So he added a little tremor to his voice.

"F-finished? Do I g-get to s-speak now?"

The demon casually waved that huge maul in a magnanimous go-ahead gesture.

Heath drew a little confidence from the scent of the mugwort in his still-burning incense.

"Look, do I even get to know the *name* of the demon who wants so badly to kill me slowly?"

"I am Valteleth, President and commander of sixty-six legions."

"Right then," Heath said, letting his voice firm up again, "Valteleth. What I started to say was that *you* may be too busy playing with your food to bother killing Colin, but what's there to stop your buddies here from having a little Colin-roast of their own?"

"Don't do this, Heath," said Colin, looking just about as angry as Heath had ever seen him. Anger added more gray to the eyes under those furrowed brows, and the set of his jaw almost looked impressive for someone so skinny.

But Heath didn't have time to answer, he was waiting for the demon to finish looking him over and speak.

"These others are mine to call and mine to order about, in the name of great Lucifuge Rofocale himself. Any bargain I strike with you binds them as well."

"Lovely," Heath said, "assuming it's true. Why don't you just prove that to me right now?"

That got past the leer to actual suspicion in those orange eyes.

"How?"

"Simple," Heath said with a smile. "Order them not to attack me or mine until you order them otherwise. Might help my friend here relax a little bit, and I can tell you it certainly would help convince me to offer you a deal."

Valteleth looked unconvinced, so Heath continued.

"This is, by the way, the only way Drake will let you get away with killing me so slowly. He's trying to make a name for himself around town as well as getting me back for showing him up. He doesn't just want me dead, he wants me dead by dusk or something like that. Doesn't he?"

The demon nodded, only once, but decisive.

"Right. So if you're as much a stickler for keeping your bargains as you *say* you are, you'll have to kill me fast to make Drake happy. If you try to do otherwise, he'll hit you with his whammy stick or whatever."

"Blasting rod," Colin said. "They call it a blasting rod."

"Right." Heath shook his head slowly. "Blasting rod. Sounds uncomfortable to me."

"Very well," Valteleth said, and the others all turned to give their chief a look. Heath couldn't see them as clearly, not with his spirit eyes closed, but he had the general impression they did not look pleased with this development.

"In the name of Lucifuge Rofocale, and in the name of He Whom We All Serve, I constrain and bind you all against striking, assaulting, or harassing our target until *I myself* give you clearance. Understood?"

Heath couldn't exactly see what rippled through those dozen demons, nor could he quite hear it, but he had the distinct impression that it was unwilling acquiescence.

Valteleth was not quite finished, though, and it turned to look at Heath as it continued.

"However—"

Heath didn't wait for it to finish.

He had a demon trap all set up and ready. All he had to do was get a demon into it.

Of course, it was a trap set for a legionnaire, not a *president*.

But Heath didn't have a lot of choices.

———

ON HIS SIDE, HEATH HAD THE RED CHALK TRIANGLE. THE SO-CALLED Triangle of Art, which apparently was a thing with demons. He had a good, compelling incense, but it was set up for a weak compulsion. A trickle of a draw, when he really needed something stronger to snatch that ugly red demon with the bruise-colored fur.

But he did have that skull candle demon trap. Yes, he'd built it for a lower class of demon, as it were, but Heath always erred on the side of a tad more *oomph* than he needed. Might not be enough, but better than nothing.

He also had a little something extra in his pockets, because Heath was a big believer in being ready for problems he never wanted to have. He had his backpack too, but there was no time to go digging for any of the other little tricks that might have come to his aid just then.

However, he did have himself, which was, at the end of the day, the best asset he could ever bring to the table.

On the other side, a big nasty of a demon, with enough power rippling out of it that a man used to looking at the strange side of the world — which Heath was — could see it full-on even when he wasn't trying to look.

For not the first time, and certainly for not the last time, Heath felt that fleeting wish that he'd never had to take up the path of the conjure man.

But now was not the time for such thoughts.

"However," Valteleth said, and before it could continue Heath leapt onto what might have been his only opportunity to survive this encounter.

He slipped his eyes into the *compelling gaze*, and slammed every bit of compulsion he could into those orange sparkly eyes. To supplement that compulsion he threw an entire packet of his own blend of *bend-over* powder, which any root worker will tell you is just about the strongest do-my-bidding concoction anybody can make.

No honey to Heath's tones this time, as he demanded obedience through the smoke of his incense.

"Valteleth, get your big ugly ass into that skull!"

The furry demon held its maul between itself and Heath like a shield, but Heath could see strain in those orange eyes.

"Betrayal," it managed through clenched teeth. "K—"

"Silence!" Heath yelled. He let the word hang a moment before saying, "You aren't in charge here. I am."

He could feel its will pressing against his own now. The demon was rallying its defenses.

Pressure in Heath's head like a slab of stone on his skull. He was clenching his own teeth. Breaths so fast and deep he could have inflated a basketball. Sweat drenched him now, but cold shivered across his spine.

"I said," he growled, "Get. Your. Ugly. Ass. In. That. Skull."

More pressure pounding his head from every direction at once.

Squeezing him. Heath had lost the element of surprise, and this thing wasn't just tough.

It was winning.

"*Heath*," Colin said, when Heath went to one knee. Poor Colin. No way to help. Not something like this.

That onyx jackal face was grinning now. Leering.

Pain, like waves from Heath's temples and spreading down his body.

His fingers dug through his pockets for the only vial he carried in his pockets.

By the time his fingers found what they wanted, Heath was on both knees. His ears rang with an ugly clatter. His heart pounded as though he'd been trying to push a semi up this damned hill.

Only the red chalk triangle stood between Heath and Valteleth now, with his purple skull sitting in the center.

"How?" Valteleth said, a thread of triumph running through its cat-shriek of a voice, "How did you ever think you could best me at willpower?"

Heath thumbed the cap off his vial of holy water and flung every drop at that demon.

"The devils also believe, and tremble!" he shouted adding faith to his struggle.

Faith and Heath had an odd kind of relationship. He'd been raised Catholic, and he'd come to learn over the years that more than a little Vodou had been included alongside that Catholicism. But Vodou and Catholicism often went hand-in-hand.

Still, outside of those early years with his family, especially his grandma, Heath didn't practice Vodou. And he'd been a lapsed Catholic for a long time now.

And yet it's true, a man who walks the path of conjure doesn't walk alone. There are saints and spirits walking alongside him, and somewhere up above there's a God keeping a distant, cursory eye on things. Heath took a more Unitarian approach to his relationship with the Almighty nowadays, but that relationship was still there.

And faith was a whole lot easier to find, on his knees before an actual demon.

So coming from Heath, that holy water and that little piece of scripture bit into Valteleth like a thousand fire ants spreading across its chest.

Valteleth howled in pain.

For a moment — just for a moment — Valteleth's attention was on the pain and not on Heath.

A tiny whisper of an opportunity, but Heath made his living in the whisper between certain death and escape.

"Get your ass in that skull!" he yelled, throwing everything he had left against the demon's willpower.

And that willpower broke.

Valteleth probably didn't actually turn into a stream of smoke like some television genie, but it did flow into the skull, maul and all.

The skull kicked and twitched there in the red triangle. Like the demon was trying to break free.

Heath dug through his backpack just as fast as he could, what with the world starting to get all ... fuzzy around the edges.

Dark, too. It was getting dark way too early.

He found what he was looking for though. A vial of *bend-over* oil made from the same mixture as that powdered packet had been.

Heath dumped the whole thing on that skull, letting its extra juice seep into every binding, every sigil, and every symbol he'd worked into the purple wax. Kicking the power of that candle up a notch or two, at least for a little while.

Pins and needles all through his fingers and hands now. Consciousness was slipping away. He'd overextended again, pushed himself too hard against that demon.

Heath bit the inside of his cheek. Gave himself something physical to remind him of his body. Help him find himself for at least a few important moments here.

And through the oil on that skull, and taking advantage of the other prep-work that had gone into that candle's making, Heath spoke to Valteleth..

"Now you just sit there quietly until I tell you to do something else."

The skull stopped trembling. Heath started listing to one side.

Colin was suddenly there, catching Heath under the shoulders.

No. Heath did not have time to pass out. That was a luxury. He had work to do.

So Heath let Colin support him as he brought himself back from the edge.

He focused on the grind of rocks and dirt under his knees. He focused on the shiver of the breeze across his sweaty body, here in the shade where the late afternoon sun couldn't warm him. The fading smell of the incense. The sounds of the traffic, moving along at a brisker clip up the street to his right.

And most of all, Heath let himself breathe. Nice and slow and deep. In one-two-three, hold one-two-three, out one-two-three, hold one-two-three, repeat.

Heath kept that up, and the blackness at the edge of his vision began receding. And the pins-and-needles feeling in his fingers and hands, that started fading too.

The world got clearer around Heath now, and since he was more obviously stable, Colin let go of Heath's shoulders.

Heath looked up.

A dozen demons still faced him.

———

Heath couldn't quite see the remaining demons, but he could see the heat-ripples of their presence, and he could tell that all twelve of the suckers had their spears raised and ready to throw.

"You want to take the ones on the left?" Colin asked.

Heath shook his head and stood up. He clapped the dust off his knees like he had all the time in the world.

"Now listen here," he said, shaking his finger at the demons like he was talking to naughty children. "You got no business raising those spears at me. You heard your boss. You don't get to attack me until *he himself* gives you the go-ahead. And I'm pretty sure we all know that's not happening anytime soon."

Heath gave the demons a moment to process that.

"So, the way I see it, you all are in a bit of a pickle. You've got an order to come kill me, and an order to do no such thing. At least, not until you're given the high sign." Heath smiled. "In fact, I think your boss here" — Heath pointed to the skull candle — "did more than order you. He *constrained* you. I'm thinking that's an even bigger deal."

The demons didn't say anything, but they didn't attack either.

"So, you don't get to kill me. Not today, anyway. And I don't think any one of you wants to go back to Drake and get a face full of blasting rod for not doing your job, when you guys are just soldiers stuck between countermanding orders. I mean, that's not really fair, now is it?"

Curiosity. Heath couldn't exactly have explained how he could tell, but he was sure he was feeling something like curiosity coming off of those demons.

"I know, I know. You want me to get to the point. Well, I'd be happy to do so. I just wanted to make sure we were all on the same page first. Wouldn't do for us to have any ... misunderstandings, when really I just want to do you all a favor."

"Favor?"

The one on Heath's far right did the talking. Had a deep voice that probably would have been good for singing.

"Of course, a favor. After all, it's not your fault you're after my hide. Some no-good human sorcerer summoned you here and bound you to his service. And it's not your fault you can't fulfill that service, because I tricked your boss into binding you not to."

Heath gave those demonic ripples the winningest smile he could manage.

"So, maybe I'm part of the reason you guys are in this fix, but let's face it — I don't owe you anything, either. You *were* coming to kill me, after all. No skin off my nose if you all get a double-dose of the blasting rod for failure."

"What is this favor?"

Heath allowed himself a long, slow breath to keep the triumph out of his smile.

"It's like this. Instead of you guys suffering such a nasty fate, I could dismiss you all. Just send you back to Hell, or wherever it is you came from."

Another ripple through his listeners, and this one felt more positive. As though they liked the idea.

"But here's the thing. If I'm going to do you guys a favor, you will owe *me* a favor too. Fair is fair."

"We cannot refuse to kill you, should the opportunity arise."

"Of course not." Heath heaved a dramatic sigh. "Honestly, it's like we're not speaking the same language. *I get it*. This isn't your fault, any more than it's mine. It's Drake's, and it's Valteleth's. I'm just stuck in the middle, same as you guys. So I'd never ask you anything so—"

"What then?"

"Simple. If you guys get free to try to kill me, or you catch wind of any other demons on the job, you give me ... say ... a twenty-four warning of who and how."

"Only us. One dismissal does not balance against monitoring other demons on your behalf."

"Fair enough," Heath said, though he swore on the inside. That would have been a coup. "I dismiss each of you, and you each agree to give me twenty-four-hour notice if you're going to attempt to kill me, and that notice must include how."

"It is agreed."

Heath waited for the ripple of agreement to spread all down the line.

He dug into his backpack for a packet of *vanish* powder, a concoction all his own. He'd designed it as a general spook-be-gone, but it had worked on a marquis of Hell, so it would work on these guys too.

Heath scattered the *vanish* powder at them and yelled, "Now go home, all of you!"

Peace. A moment of actual peace that felt like purest bliss.

And just like that the western meadowlarks started singing again.

"Whew," Heath said, and laughter bubbled out of him. He felt so good right then he couldn't help bending forward, hands on his knees, and just giving himself to laughter for a minute or two.

"Damn it, Heath," Colin said, but that wasn't enough to break through the laughter.

"Come on!" Colin said. "Enough with the hysteria."

Hysteria? That sounded like an unfair assessment, but it did get Heath to slow his chuckle to a halt like the diminishing trickle of water out of a tap that's slowly turned off.

Meanwhile, traffic was moving along pretty well on its way up and down the hill, and the afternoon sunlight was beginning to fade toward twilight. Had to be at least a little after seven in the evening then.

Explained the complaining rumble in Heath's belly. Hadn't eaten in too long, and he always needed a meal after pulling a trick like that. Probably needed to wait until he secured his catch a little more tightly, though.

The breeze had turned cooler, and it was carrying the woodsy scent from the park to Heath's right.

But Colin, Colin looked cross. How unfair was that? Heath had just pulled off one hell of a trick, and here his only witness didn't seem to appreciate the finesse involved.

Heath picked up the skull. He could feel Valteleth inside it, furious but unable to act for the time being. The spells on the skull weren't binding the demon president's will the way they would have a lesser demon, but they were trying and — bolstered by the *bend-over* oil — having at least some success.

Heath held up the skull and smiled at Colin.

"All right," Colin conceded, "I admit. I don't ever want to play poker with you or buy a used car from you."

"I'm sure I could get you a good deal on one."

"My point is," Colin continued, "will you at least concede that I was

right and this was a stupid idea? You almost got yourself killed, and for what?"

Heath gave the skull a shake.

"A president, Colin. I've got a president bound in here. I couldn't have asked for a better inside informant on what Drake's up to and how." Heath smiled. "Plus. Remember what I was saying about gaining resources by denying them to my enemy?"

"Nariko's right," Colin said with a sigh. "You're—"

"If you say 'dumb in all the wrong ways,'" Heath said, no doubt looking just as cross with Colin as he felt in that moment, "you and I are going to have words."

Colin tried to say something, but Heath wasn't ready to listen.

"You think carefully about what you say next. You think about the fact that these demons were coming to kill me, whether I met them here or whether they eventually found their way past my defenses. This way *I* picked the time and place for that confrontation. I bound the leader, and got another dozen to not only not kill me, but give me twenty-four-hour notice if they're ever free to try again."

"That *was* a pretty good move." Colin didn't look happy about saying it, but at least he said it. "But this didn't exactly go according to plan, now did it?"

"And what do you think my first question for this president is going to be?"

Colin didn't bother answering. Just got a chagrined look on his face. That was good though, so Heath gave a little.

"Look. I don't like these risks any more than you do. Honest." Heath wrapped the skull candle in his pure white handkerchief and tucked it into his backpack. "But I can't just lay low while Drake plays Battleship until he eventually sinks me."

"I guess not."

Colin actually looked a little guilty then. Heath could tell by the slight hang to his head and slump to his shoulders.

"I'm not Nariko," Heath said. "I don't pack the kind of punch that lets me square off against any problem in my path. I need to be a little

... sneakier. That means taking risks sometimes. If you can't handle that, that's cool. Fights like this, they're not your thing."

"I'm not abandoning you." Colin shook his head so hard that Heath was surprised Colin's blond hair didn't crack like a whip. Colin had a smile when he was done though, as though he'd shaken off whatever was bothering him. "Come on. Let's get moving before something else comes looking for you."

Heath extinguished his incense, buried the coal in the salt, and tossed the bedpan into his backpack, then zipped it closed. He rubbed away the chalk dust triangle by scuffling his boat shoes through the dirt, then took a quick look around.

Didn't see any of the local spirits keeping an eye on him, but his spirit eyes were closed. They might well have been watching the whole thing. Good. Heath dug into the outside pocket of his backpack for a blue glass bottle of pure, clean water that he'd blessed himself.

He held up the bottle, made a show of uncapping it, then said, "Hey, you local spirits. You of the rocks and the dirt, you of the asphalt and the trees and the blackberry brambles, you of the birds, the sky, the breeze, and all the rest of you. Thank you for letting me use this place. And thank you for keeping quiet about it. I honestly hope I haven't done anything to offend any of you, but if I did, please accept my sincere apologies."

Heath poured out a little of the clear water.

"This is for you. Come, take and enjoy."

He poured out a little more.

"Come, take and enjoy, with my compliments and thanks."

He poured out a little more.

"Come, take and enjoy, and maybe think well of me when I come by again."

By then Colin had his Saturn running and ready, and the passenger side door hanging open, just waiting for Heath.

Heath re-capped the bottle and slipped it back into its pocket in the backpack, then joined Colin in the car.

"Ready?" Colin asked.

Heath nodded as he fastened his seatbelt.

Colin turned and, without a moment's hesitation, turned left to join the traffic down the hill. He just pulled his car out into a gap that Heath could tell had to be there for him.

So maybe Colin didn't enchant his car, exactly, but clearly he had a few driving tricks up his sleeve. Still, that wasn't the question on Heath's mind as they drove down into the main streets of Portland.

"Your middle name is *Amadeus*?"

4

FIVE MINUTES OF TEASING COLIN ABOUT HIS MIDDLE NAME WAS apparently all it took to get the facts out of him while they drove down the hills of West Portland in Colin's Saturn sedan.

"All right," Colin said at last, with a sheepish grin. "I changed my middle name *to* Amadeus."

"You wanted your initials to call you a cad?"

"Better that than a bounder." Colin shook his head and took a right turn where Heath expected a left. "What can I say? It *was* Iollan, which I was never fond of. Plus, you try growing up with your brothers calling you El Cid and see how you like it."

"Don't have any siblings." Not living, anyway, but Heath kept that part to himself. He also kept one hand inside his backpack, holding the purple skull candle in its white handkerchief, which was now damp with *bend-over* oil. Just a little extra warning, in case anything started to give.

"Well it sucks." Colin took a left now that he definitely shouldn't have taken. They were on Burnside, which might have taken them to Powell's City of Books, or across the river, or to any number of restaurants ... but going this direction it wouldn't take them back to Heath's place.

"When they started calling me 'Yo! Lynn!' I resolved I'd change it at the first chance I got. Then, when I was eighteen I was heavy into transcribing Mozart for the guitar—"

"Colin, just where are we going?"

"My place," Colin said like it was the most obvious thing in the world.

"What, Nariko's out of town, so you figured…"

"For *that* I might risk her wrath, if I thought you'd go for it." Colin winked at him. "No, I figured that if Drake's homing in on you, why not get you someplace safe where you're also not at home? I think I proved last month that my wards are pretty impressive."

Heath thought that over as Colin eased them through the evening traffic. Burnside was a nice, wide street, but a popular one. Between tourists and locals — not to mention more damned bicyclists — it could be slow going at times.

Apparently this wasn't one of those times. Heath had barely realized they were approaching Powell's when they were scooting past that huge, weird statue across the street from the famous bookstore. The statue that looked like a whisk suspended brush-up on a tripod.

And Heath could tell their speed was not simple coincidence.

A little emphasis to the fact that Colin's wards had kept everyone but Uncle Andre from finding Heath. And Uncle Andre, well, Heath wasn't sure anything could keep *him* out.

"That's a fair point," Heath said, "but most of my best resources are at my place."

"Are the ingredients for lamb kebabs with onions and peppers at your place?"

Heath's stomach rumbled loud enough to answer for him.

"Thought not," Colin said with a smile. "We can head to your place later if you insist, but if I can't help you with anything else, I can at least make sure you get a good meal. I know how much your work takes out of you."

And just like that, they were pulling up outside Colin's two-bedroom condo, part of a little development where the grass was always green and neat, the hedges were arborvitae and uniform in height, and Colin's siding was painted electric blue...

Electric blue? The last time Heath had seen Colin's place, the exterior had been an adobe brown, fitting in with the color scheme of the rest of the development.

As Colin killed the engine, he turned an expectant smile to Heath. No doubt waiting for the obvious question.

Heath had a different topic in mind first.

"Tricky work," he said with a raised eyebrow. "Getting us here that fast and smooth. Barely picked up the juju myself, and I was in the car with you."

"Horus power," Colin said, letting his smile widen even more. "You're not the only one who can be subtle."

Heath quirked a lop-sided smile, but let his tones get serious.

"I don't doubt your skills. You know that."

"So you better start letting me in on your plans then. What good is having friends if you won't let us help you?"

Colin didn't wait for an answer this time, just got out of the car, leaving Heath to hop out and trail after him.

"Hard to believe a man who lives in an electric blue house can call himself subtle."

"Never said *I* was subtle. Just that my magic can be. Why do you think there was a loophole in the H.O.A. bylaws that let me pull this off?"

Colin opened the door and they went inside.

Heath had thought he'd be used to Colin's place by now, but Colin kept surprising him.

The entryway was still cherry wood, and the carpeting in the living room was still the color of sea foam. But the couch, loveseat and pair of recliners were new. The old ones had been pale blue, but these were dark blue. Maybe indigo. The same walnut coffee table sat between them, with fanned magazines about architecture as well as music.

The wall-mounted television was a fifty-inch now, to go with the surround sound speakers set into the eggshell-white walls.

Abstract oil paintings on the walls, alive with rainbow colors, all the work of local artists. On a stand in the corner waited an acoustic guitar that Heath knew was worth more than Colin's Saturn.

Off to the left were carpeted stairs leading up to Colin's bedroom and the bedroom-cum-music-studio he'd set up. Off to the right was the fancy dining room, done in dark woods above cherry hardwood floor, and beyond that the kitchen.

The place smelled like homemade potpourri. Heath could pick out violet, lavender and orange blossom, which worked better together than he would have expected. Had to have had something to do with the base holding them together. Cotton, if Heath's nose read it right.

"You've been redecorating."

"Needed a change after your uncle's 'visit' last month."

Nothing to say to that, so Heath headed for the kitchen.

Just as elegant as the dining room, the kitchen had a cherry hardwood floor and swirls of blue and pink through its white marble counters. The cabinets were white oak, to match the hand-carved table and chairs in the breakfast nook, and the stools that tucked into the end of the kitchen's center island.

Heath set his backpack on the center island.

"Mind if I get some work done while you start on dinner?"

"Yes."

Heath did a double-take. Colin was looking at him with the kind of sober expression that didn't suit him. Enough to make Heath a little uneasy, here in Colin's place of power.

"Colin," Heath said slowly, "you do realize that if I don't do something to strengthen the bindings on that skull candle, you're going to have a demon loose in your house."

"There's something we need to talk about first."

Heath sighed, folded his arms and leaned back against the counter. He didn't like this one bit, but Colin had certainly earned the right to speak his piece.

"I'm not kidding. You're going to have to let me in on your plans.

And let me give you more magical aid than just emergency clean up or distracting the unenlightened."

Heath blinked at that. "Unenlightened?"

"I hate terms like 'normals' and 'mundanes.' People aren't normal or mundane, just because they don't know the kinds of things we know."

"Huh. I'd call them the lucky ones, because between the two of us, I don't feel all that enlightened my own self."

That got a snicker out of Colin, and seemed to take some of the tension out of him. He reached into his brushed steel refrigerator for a pair of strong Teufelsbrau IPAs, popped the caps, and handed one to Heath.

Heath's belly rumbled.

"Not to put too much of a rush on the chef," he said, "but this beer may hit me too hard to get much work done if I don't get something in my stomach soon."

"So agree to share your plans with me. Agree to let me *actually* help you instead of this token aid bullshit. You're one of my best friends, Heath, and someone's trying to kill you."

"And the whole community knows it," Heath said with a grimace. "If I let you help—"

"Fuck how it looks and fuck Drake. Drake made this to the *death*. So you tell me if I'm wrong, but that means this can only end with one of you in a casket."

Heath suspected he could find a third option, if only because he considered third options his personal specialty. But the point was fair, so he nodded.

"Then let the community figure out that if anyone tries to fuck with you, even when Nariko's out of town, you've still got friends who'll put their lives on the line for you."

"You think Drake waited until Nariko was out of town?"

"Hell yes. I sure would have."

Heath chuckled, but he pulled Colin into a hug.

"Thank you. Really. I appreciate everything you do for me, and everything you've done."

"And?" said Colin, not willing to let Heath go yet.

"And I'll let you in on my plans and strategies in this little war, and I'll let you help with both. And in both this case and the future, I won't be afraid to call on help."

"Then you're welcome." Colin released the hug, and clinked beer bottles with Heath. "To Drake's downfall."

That, Heath would drink to.

COLIN STARTED COOKING WHILE HEATH MADE A PHONE CALL, THEN GOT down to work.

In short order, Colin had the kitchen smelling so good that Heath's stomach was rumbling nonstop. Colin had finally shoved a bowl of honey roasted cashews in front of Heath, to cut down on the noise.

Heath just picked up the small, crystal bowl like a coffee mug and tipped cashews into his mouth as he worked. The taste went well with the strong IPA, and while the nuts may have sated stomach enough to still the rumble, they only whetted his appetite.

Focusing on what he was doing helped.

He started by inventorying what he had — a reasonable amount of supplies, but he'd want to get home and refresh his herbs, roots and incenses by tomorrow at the latest. Not to mention getting his hands on a few other things.

Heath sprinkled a little confusion powder in a circle on a section of the white marble center island that Colin wasn't using. If this demon president managed to get away from Heath, they would have at least a moment's breathing room before it attacked.

Fortunately, Colin did his chopping and seasoning on another counter, only using the center island's burners when he was ready to cook. And right now he had what smelled like perfectly seasoned lamb pre-cooking in the oven.

Rosemary, oregano, basil and a hint of garlic had that lamb watering Heath's mouth, so he munched down one more mouthful of honey-roasted cashews. Then he dusted off his hands and got serious.

He set the white handkerchief — spotted with *bend-over* oil — down in the center of the confusion powder. Heath unfolded the handkerchief, and immediately he could feel Valteleth vibrating within its confines. Trying to batter its way free by will alone

"Right, now," Heath said, "Valteleth, you and me, we need to talk. So I give you permission to show me a wee ghostie face, for purposes of communication with me and Colin only. Otherwise you are to remain perfectly still until I give you permission to do something else."

A small jackal's head, black as onyx and only a little more transparent, eased into view above the purple skull. The jackal's orange eyes still sparked, but their color was muddied and subdued.

Colin snickered. "He looks like some goth's bust of Anubis."

"Thou canst—" Valteleth began, cut Heath cut him off.

"Oh, cut the Shakespeare crap," Heath said, shaking his head. "Maybe the ceremonialists who love you guys so much go in for that kind of archaic pomposity, but me, I'm just a simple root worker. And I like plain English just fine, thank you very much."

"You cannot contain me. The sorcerer has not yet been born who can bind me for any length of time..."

"You can can the bravado while you're at it," Heath said. "Seriously. Look around you. Do you see any Latin? Any Hebrew? Any lists of angels and archangels, or synonyms for the Almighty? Do you?"

"I do not, but that changes nothing. I—"

"That changes *everything*." Heath snorted and shook his head. "I'm not the kind of guy who calls up folks like you, and I'm not the kind of guy interested in *keeping* folks like you."

"Why trap me within this candle then?"

"Now one answer to that should be obvious. You were trying to kill me. And me, I've gotten pretty attached to living. Some people might argue that I don't do a very good job of it, but it's what I know and I'm used to it."

"Implying that there is an inobvious answer?"

Heath smiled. "Isn't there always?"

"Magician, you are clever, but I have my mission and will do everything within my power to fulfill it."

"And that mission is to kill me, yes?"

For just a moment, those dull orange eyes flared bright.

Heath tried not to let that trouble him, but he could feel a little sweat breaking out on the back of his neck and under his arms. He needed to either get this done quickly, or figure out a way to bind the damned thing before it broke free.

But worrying wasn't going to help, so Heath took a moment to focus on the masterful way Colin chopped onions and peppers. Maybe not as good as Heath, who whittled and chopped and carved for a great many reasons, but good enough to be on a cooking show.

And Heath had every intention of living to eat Colin's lamb kebabs.

"So," Heath said, "if that's the extent of it, then there are all kinds of ways you and I can help each other."

"Your trick with the powder may have worked on my legionnaires, but it will not work on me."

"Worked on a marquis," Heath said with a shrug. "Samigina. Figure it'll work just as well on a president like you."

"Marquis outranks president," Colin said, without slowing down his chopping. "In Hell, anyway."

Heath smiled again.

"You mistake me, magician," Valteleth said. "You might banish me, but I have my orders. Send me home and I shall return with twice as many legionnaires. I shall slice through these wards as easily as I shall slice through your stomach lining. And I shall not be tricked a second time."

The anger in Valteleth's voice shook the wineglasses Colin kept hanging from a cabinet. The sound of their chiming like tiny evil laughter.

Heath waited for the chiming to stop.

"While I admire your work ethic," Heath said, "I'd like to think we could come to an understanding. I mean, you've already proven you're ready to deal."

"I will not bargain while trapped."

"Weird," Heath said to Colin. "And here I thought that would be the time it would be most likely to deal. Oh, well."

"Need any carving tools?" Colin asked as he swept the sliced onions into one pile and the peppers into another.

"Nope," Heath said, pulling a multi-tool out of his pocket. "Always carry a set, just in case."

Heath started reaching for the skull.

"What sort of deal did you have in mind?" Valteleth asked.

Heath kept the smile off his face and his voice on the innocent side of unconcerned. But he stopped his hand short of the confusion powder circle.

"Doesn't matter, right? You don't deal while—"

"What. Sort. Of. Deal?"

"Well," Heath said, drawing out the word much longer than he needed to, "it seems to me that you probably know a good deal about Drake's defenses and maybe even a little bit about his plans. If you were to let me in on these things, swearing to their truth by everything that would compel a demon such as yourself, then..." — Heath bobbed his head back and forth while he pretended to think — "I could see my way to making it look like you're trying to kill me while you head back to Hell for a little r-and-r, as it were."

"You believe that there could be rest and recreation in Hell?"

"Look, I don't care what you *do* there, as long as you're there, and not trying to kill me."

"So you receive information and a temporary reprieve from any attempts by me to kill you."

The demon wasn't finished, but Heath jumped in.

"Any attempts by you or at your instruction, command, or cause."

"Very well, any attempts to kill you myself or through the actions of another. What you stand to gain is clear. But what do I stand to gain beyond freedom from this confining candle?"

"I figure a noble demon such as yourself isn't too overfond of being ordered around by the likes of Drake. What with all that summoning and compelling, not even giving you the opportunity to strike a bargain with him. This way, you get to *not* do your job, thus sticking it to the human."

"Foolish human. We obey because of arrangements older than you would believe. And I enjoy killing." The jackal's mouth spread in a grin that had no business on a face like that. "And in your case, I shall enjoy it a great deal."

"So," Heath said, "I'm not getting the sense that you're really interested in bargaining."

"You have nothing to offer me that I could, or would, accept."

"So, you're saying this little thing between us is going to come down to me trying to bind you and you trying to break free and kill me?"

"I believe I know which of our wills will break first."

The doorbell rang, an eight-note chime that was new, yet sounded vaguely familiar.

"Oh, do excuse me," Heath said. "In the spirit of Colin's Heath-asks-for-help policy, I've invited a little someone over who'd just *love* to meet you."

WHEN HEATH OPENED COLIN'S FRONT DOOR, THE MAN WAITING ON THE threshold wasn't wearing a brown robe. That was almost enough to make Heath think this was some solicitor, but he took an extra moment to give the visitor a once-over before saying anything.

Despite the summer heat, this man wore black wool slacks and a black, long-sleeved, button-up shirt. And every button on that shirt was fastened. The shirt was tucked into the pants, and a simple black leather belt cinched the man's hefty waist.

"Hefty" wasn't quite right though, the more Heath looked at him. Not with those broad shoulders and rough, calloused hands. More like football-player big. In fact, adding those things to the slightly olive complexion and the Roman nose, Heath had a fleeting thought that the guy might be a Mafioso. Maybe even sent by the Lammergeyer.

But the visitor had a ring of black hair around a big, tonsured bald spot on his scalp.

Just like the other monks Heath had met from the Protective Order of Saint Benedict.

"Brother Antonio?" Heath said, extending his hand.

"Yes," Brother Antonio said in a gentle tenor. "Pleased to meet you, Mr. Cyr. Brother Theodopolis speaks quite highly of you."

When they shook hands, Brother Antonio's grip was as gentle as his voice. As though he didn't have any challenge in him at all.

Heath suddenly worried that Brother Theodopolis had sent the wrong man to offer aid.

"Say hi to him for me," Heath said as he led the monk into Colin's house, heading for the kitchen. "Not sure I'm ready to let him kick my ass at chess, but I do appreciate his offers."

"You should consider them. Brother Theodopolis enjoys helping others improve their games. You'd get better and he would get a more challenging opponent."

Brother Antonio looked Colin's house over as they crossed the living room and dining room, but he didn't seem to be taking in the view the way most people would: assessing, looking for points of difference and similarity with their own tastes.

Instead, Heath would have sworn that in the brief walk from the front door to Colin's kitchen, Brother Antonio had already drawn accurate conclusions about who Colin was as a person.

Maybe this monk was not someone to invite over for tea.

In the kitchen, Colin was butchering a Peter Gabriel song into "Shock the Demon" while frying peppers and onions along with lamb cubes at temperatures hot enough to sear the lamb. The aroma was heavenly.

Before Heath could say anything about the demon, Brother Antonio brushed past him and knelt to look up at the not-quite-transparent jackal head floating above the skull candle. And if Heath was not mistaken, Brother Antonio was examining the skull candle as well, even sniffing to get a sense of the oils glistening on the purple skull.

"No taunts, demon?" Brother Antonio asked with what sounded like genuine surprise, as he stood again.

"My fault," Heath said, double-tapping his chest before turning to Valteleth and saying, "This is Brother Antonio. You may communicate with him as well, but you may deal or bargain with only me."

"Half a sorcerer and half a priest." Valteleth managed to drip scorn into each word. "Between the two of you, you're still half an opponent."

Heath wanted to ask about the half-a-priest comment, but decided against letting the demon divide them.

"This is President Valteleth, you said?" Brother Antonio looked over at Heath until he nodded. "And yet I do not see his sigil carved into the candle."

"Was just about to get down to business."

"Then the Lord has guided me here in time to stop you."

"Wait," Heath said, but Brother Antonio had no intention of waiting.

He pulled a silver crucifix from the pocket of his pants that may have looked small, but was potent enough that even halfway across the kitchen Heath felt guilty about how long it had been since he'd attended a mass.

And that was quite some time ago.

The Latin came next. The *pater noster* was expected, but Brother Antonio continued into something that sounded vaguely familiar to Heath. Almost like...

...like an exorcism.

"Whoa!" he said, quick-stepping across the room to grab Brother Antonio by the free arm.

Brother Antonio kept right on reciting. Meanwhile Valteleth looked almost ash gray instead of onyx, and the jackal-head's orange eyes lost what little sparkle they'd had.

"Stop!" Heath said. "I need this thing."

Too late though. Brother Antonio finished with a flourish and the jackal head swirled away into nothingness.

The skull candle was empty now. Heath could feel it.

Heath forced himself to let go of the monk's sleeve, and flared his nostrils in a slow, deep breath to stay his right hand. He had the feeling that punching a monk was not the sort of thing that the Almighty took all that kindly to, even when the punch was thrown by a lapsed Catholic who was really more of a Unitarian these days.

Well, the part of him that was Christian, anyway. The Lwa themselves kept insisting that Heath was one of their own...

But that was an issue he didn't even have time to consider right now. Getting hold of himself and not punching the monk were his priorities.

"I'm glad I got here in time," Brother Antonio said. "I could feel that the demon was on the verge of escaping."

"He was on the *verge*," Heath said, "of making a deal with me."

"So much the better."

Brother Antonio's gentle voice was really starting to grate on Heath. And it didn't help that Colin was whistling softly and trying not to be noticed, which was the way he handled things when Heath and Nariko were arguing.

And Nariko wasn't here, which was just one more thing for Heath to be upset about. Instead of being here, she was off in Japan, near one of its tallest mountains — important to her Shugendō practice, he knew — but worst of all, in some kind of mess...

Another deep breath for Heath. And then another.

"Have I done something wrong?" Brother Antonio asked Colin.

"I'm not touching that with a ten foot pole," Colin said. "And I'm not saying I don't have one."

Heath punched his palm.

"Do you know," he said quietly, "what I *went through* today to get that demon right where I had it?"

"I would imagine," Brother Antonio said, "it has caused you considerable bother, or you would not have called Brother Theodopolis."

"I didn't need rescue. I needed backup."

"Mr. Cyr, I know that it is fashionable to think of demons as neutral spirits. Equivalents of the Greek daimons. However—"

"I am fighting for my life," Heath said, tension in his quiet tones. "And that demon represented information that could mean the difference between life and death."

Brother Antonio reached out one big, callused hand and laid it gently on Heath's shoulder.

"No, Mr. Cyr. It didn't."

The monk shook his head slowly, and to his credit he didn't show a trace of pity, condescension, or any other emotion that might have set Heath off. Those brown eyes shone with only patience.

"Mr. Cyr, it is possible to constrain demons to honesty, but it is not possible to barter with them for honesty. Whatever promises it might have uttered, it would not have kept. Not unless you used the proper formulae to bring in the right angels and powers in support."

Brother Antonio looked around the kitchen.

"I see none of those things here."

"I could have—"

"Bargained with a lesser spirit? One of the troops under its command?" Brother Antonio raised his bushy salt-and-pepper eyebrows. "Yes. That you could have done and compelled it to obedience. But a greater demon such as Valteleth? With a title and province?"

Brother Antonio shook his head slowly.

"I know you do not appreciate my going straight to the exorcism, but I needed to dismiss the demon before it got free of such fetters as you managed for it."

Heath took one more slow breath to try to ignore having some of his best improvised binding work dismissed so casually. In fact, he was surprised at the lightness of his own tone when he spoke.

"Well, that's just fine. I completely understand. Mind you, *it's still going to try to kill me*, but I can always deal with that later, right?"

"Oh," Brother Antonio said, shoulders drooping forward and

head hanging, "please forgive me. I thought you understood. I would have made myself more clear in the first place—"

"Hey," Heath said, guilt gnawing at his gut for giving the monk a hard time when the guy was only doing his job. "It's all right. I dealt with it once, I can—"

"But you won't have to."

The words rushed out of Brother Antonio's mouth so fast Heath needed a moment to parse them. But before he could ask the obvious question, Brother Antonio continued.

"Such is the nature of that form of the rite of exorcism, when performed on an extant demon. The power of our Lord shattered any bindings or obligations upon the demon as it was sent back to Hell."

Heath blinked. "Really?"

"Oh yes." Brother Antonio was smiling now, and the smile had a touch of mischief to it. "And Valteleth cannot be summoned and bound on this plane again until the next anniversary of our Savior's crucifixion. You will not have to face that demon again for the better part of a year, at the minimum."

Heath smiled.

"See, Heath," Colin said from where he was finishing up skewering the kebabs, "it's good to have friends. I trust you're staying for dinner, Brother Antonio?"

FOR HEATH, FINALLY GETTING TO EAT DINNER TOOK SOME OF THE STING out of losing a potential source of information. He hadn't realized just how starved he felt until food was on the table in front of him.

To go with the lamb kebabs, Colin served homemade garlic bread (reheated from a loaf in his fridge) and more Teufelsbrau I.P.A. When they first sat down to dinner, Brother Antonio had remarked that Colin had prepared enough food for an army.

The poor monk had no idea who he was eating with.

Heath managed four kebabs and a decent-sized portion of garlic bread. He found himself regretting those honey-roasted cashews, because they kept him from eating more delicious lamb. And the lamb was perfect, done to hints of pink and so juicy Heath went through three napkins while eating. The seasoning, held together by the rosemary, brought out the subtleties in the meat, and the peppers and onions added the kind of variety that made the lamb itself even better.

Then there was the bread, so infused with garlic that Heath needed swigs from his beer to keep the garlic from overwhelming the kebabs.

Colin had a dozen kebabs himself, and half the loaf of garlic bread.

Brother Antonio contented himself with three kebabs, barely a slice of bread, and swore he couldn't have eaten another bite.

They ate without conversation, not so much as a statement as because Heath and Colin were too hungry to waste open mouths on words. Brother Antonio seemed to pick up on that, and the three settled into a companionable silence.

But once the serious business of eating was out of the way, the three of them sat back in their white oak chairs. Brother Antonio ran his hands over the carvings along the edge of the matching table.

"Amish work?"

"I know a guy," Colin said with a smile.

"Mr. Cyr," Brother Antonio started, but Heath interrupted him.

"Call me Heath, please. 'Mr. Cyr' is what people call my dad. And worse, my uncle."

"Heath then," Brother Antonio said with a broad smile. "And if you would, please call me Tony."

Heath nodded, and Tony continued.

"I know that you only called for assistance in coping with a summoned demon, but Brother Theodopolis is worried about you. He said that you're involved in some kind of duel to the death?"

"Something like that," Heath said with a grimace. "A guy declared he's going to kill me, and the way he did it pretty much says he'll succeed or die trying."

"Perhaps I could reason with him?"

Colin snickered, but Heath contented himself with a snort.

"Reason isn't Drake's long suit."

"Drake?" Tony asked, a look of pain entering his expressive brown eyes. He sat forward in his chair. "Not the man who calls himself Mandrake by any chance."

Heath nodded.

"I see." Tony sighed. "You're right, then. There's no reasoning with him. There never was."

"You know him," Colin said.

"All my life." Tony sipped at his beer. "Well, all *his* life, anyway. He's my younger brother."

"You don't look much like him," Colin said.

"My mother died when I was very young. Our father remarried, and the one you call Drake is the fruit of that union."

Hope bubbled inside Heath's chest, and he had to take a sip of beer to keep from letting it show on his face.

"Wow," Heath said, voice smooth as a used car salesman. "What was it like growing up with a guy like him? Was he the type to pull the wings off flies?"

"Not at all. Sh..." Tony glanced at Heath, then back at his beer. "Drake was quiet. Bookish. Not kind, but he had the innocence of all children."

Tony sipped his beer. Colin got so quiet he almost vanished, and Heath could hear the rapid beat of his own heart as he listened for any clue that might help him beat his declared foe.

"He resented me though," Tony continued. "I think that's why he got into black magic. Because I felt the Lord's call at a young age. I didn't know what he was into, of course. Not until it was too late. By then..." Tony looked out the window and back. "As you say, there's no reasoning with him."

"Perhaps there is, though," Heath said. "If I could find common ground with him somewhere. What can you tell me about him?"

"Nothing that will help you kill him," Tony said, and those brown eyes almost seemed to look straight through Heath. "Murder is a mortal sin. And even if it weren't, he is still my brother."

"Hey," Heath said, one hand coming up defensively, "I'm not clicking my heels together at the thought of killing anyone. Heck, it wasn't eight hours ago I was telling that very truth to a would-be client who wanted me to commit murder for her."

"You declined the job, of course."

"Hell yes. I don't kill for money. And I'd just as soon not kill because some jerk wants to off me, either. But if Drake pushes this, I may not have a choice."

"There's always a choice," Tony said.

"Well, if my 'choice' is I die or he dies, then you're going to be short one brother."

Heath tried to dramatically finish his beer, but only one swig remained. So instead he slammed down the empty and stomped back to the fridge for three more.

He brought them back to the table before opening them and passing two to the others.

All three men clinked their bottles together and drank a silent toast.

"*Hell*," Heath said, sharply enough that Colin and Tony almost spilled their beers. "I just remembered. Today's demon might not even be Drake's serious attempt to introduce me to the groundhog—"

"Groundhog?" Tony said.

"'Cause I'll be underground," Heath said. "Dead. Get it?"

Tony gave a slow nod.

"Back before I met Goldilocks, some punk hipster-wannabe passed on a threat from Drake. Said ... 'death will come for you on the third day, during the hour of Mars.'"

"Third day," Colin said. "From yesterday? Or from today? Or does he mean Tuesday, the third day of the week, which also happens to be *named* for Mars?"

"If I knew that," Heath said, "I might be able to tell you what the hour of Mars was."

"Planetary hours change day by day," Tony said, voice almost distracted. "And the third day *might* mean the third day from the initial threat, but more likely it means the third day of the current cycle which would be Saturday."

"Current cycle?" Heath asked.

"While most believe that Sunday is always the sun's day, and that the rest of the days of the week follow their nomenclature for their planetary associations, the authors of the greatest grimoires understood that this was not entirely the case. The truest planetary hours spread themselves across the days in a way that does not evenly suit our days of the week. The current planetary week began today. Probably why ... Drake issued his threat yesterday. The third day would be Saturday, and the hour of Mars would be between two and three p.m."

"See," Heath said, "he sounds pretty intent on his outcome, and loathe as I am to take a life I don't have to, I would much rather see him dead than me."

"I'm with Heath on this," Colin said. "I really, *really* don't like the idea of killing anyone. But better him than Heath."

"I don't consider the death of either an acceptable outcome," Tony said. "There must be a third option."

"I get that." Heath set down his beer. "Believe me. I really do. But third options, they don't always work out. So I need to know right now. If it comes down to me or him, which will you choose?"

Tony shook his head. "I cannot make that choice."

"What *can* you do?" Colin asked, giving Heath a look he couldn't quite interpret. Was that an attempt at a *quit-it* look?

"I can shield you from his demons while we attempt to find a peaceful solution."

Heath thought about that through a long pull of the strong beer. He shook his head.

"I'm not sure it can work that way. Everyone knows he's trying to kill me. If I just go defensive, especially letting someone else handle my defenses, that's tantamount to saying I can't beat him."

"Who cares what others think?" Tony asked, the genuine surprise of the cloistered in his eyes. "We're discussing the fate of your soul."

"My soul knows its own fate better than I ever will," Heath said.

"But this is the world I have to live in. And the people who are watching this, they're part of my world too."

"You would commit murder to avoid looking weak?"

"Not at all," Heath said. "Believe me. If I could get my ass out of this with a trick, I'd do it with a smile on my face and a song in my heart. But this guy wants to take it all the way. So if I want to stop him, I have to accept that his death is a possibility. And as far as I'm concerned, if he dies it's his own damn fault for being too stupid to issue a challenge without a reasonable out."

"You're serious," Tony said, in genuine amazement. "Can you truly be the same man who turned over *The Black Book of Saint Cyprian* because he had no interest in black magic?"

"You keep using that term. 'Black magic.'" Heath snorted and quirked a half-smile. "You know what they call the kind of magic I do? Back down around Louisiana?"

Tony shook his head.

"*Gris-gris*. It means gray-gray. As in, not black and not white." Heath raised his beer. "And it doesn't refer to skin color."

Heath sipped his beer, watching Tony. He saw conflict in the monk's posture, but he wasn't sure he understood what that conflict was.

"Look," Colin said. "Let's none of us do anything hasty here—"

"I'm not going to sit here," Heath said, "and be called a murderer or a black magician because I might be forced to kill someone in self-defense."

Tony didn't say anything. He sat there, watching Heath right back, his hands forming a triangle around the sweating beer bottle on the wooden table. Those brown eyes, they started searching Heath for something. Heath couldn't feel them probe, but he was sure that was what was happening.

"You said it yourself," Heath said to fill the silence. "He can't be reasoned with. And he wants me dead. I'd make him leave town, but that won't be enough. He'll keep sending his demons anyway. I could hurt him. I could hurt him bad. But if I don't kill him, he's just going to keep coming."

Heath drank a long pull from his beer and slammed the bottle down.

"Hell. If I could get the right links, I might even be able to bind away his magic. Leave him with an impotent blasting rod and not a single demon answering his calls. But a guy like Drake, he'd probably just come after me with a pipe bomb."

"A pipe bomb," Colin said, "we could handle."

"Then..." Heath started, then trailed off and shook his head again. They just weren't getting the point. Why weren't they getting the point?

Heath was out of things he wanted to say, and his beer was empty again, but he didn't want another one. So he sat there and fidgeted, and tried to resist getting in Tony's face over the staring.

"Heath Cyr," Tony said at last, and his tones seemed to echo in Colin's kitchen. "In the names of Michael, Gabriel, Rafael and Uriel, I charge you to tell me truly: will you accept a peaceful solution to this conflict, if we can find it?"

To Heath's irritation, a golden peace settled over him and words poured out of his mouth before he had time to consider them.

"If we can find a solution that doesn't ruin me in this community? Absolutely."

"Well," Tony said in a surprised tone. "The community really does matter to you here."

"He has more friends," Colin said, "than he's willing to accept."

"Very well then," Tony said, nodding his head slowly. "I shall stay and help you find a nonlethal solution to your conflict."

"On one condition," Heath said, and he knew the grin on his face looked menacing. "You ever do that to me again, I'll make sure you get to go meet each of those angels in person a whole lot sooner than you expect to."

Tony smiled, and just for a moment he looked like the Mafioso Heath had thought he might be.

"I accept your terms."

TWO HOURS OF FRUITLESS DISCUSSION BROUGHT THEM NO CLOSER TO any plans that Heath thought had a chance in hell of working. And given his opponent, "chance in Hell" sounded about right.

Colin was right about one thing though: having friends was better than going it alone. Going it alone led to viewpoints like Uncle Andre's. One man against the world and anything goes. Not the way Heath wanted to live.

But while help and camaraderie were definitely good things, having to discuss his plans with people who just didn't get the way he worked was starting to look like a crash course in frustration and anger.

But Heath let it go. By the time he left Colin's house that evening, close to eleven o'clock, he might not have had any solid plans of attack but he'd gotten both Colin and Tony to admit that Heath was going about things in a way that made sense. Strong defenses while gathering information, then striking at an unexpected time, from an unexpected angle.

And given the way the day had gone, getting *any* kind of admission out of those two felt like a victory.

Twice in one day, Heath had had to convince someone that he was not out to commit murder. Just what was wrong with the world that he had to prove such a thing not just once, but *twice*? In *one day*?

Heath was beginning to get the distinct feeling that one or more of the Lwa were having fun at his expense. A Ghede, maybe, or one of the Barons. Pranksters each, in their own way, and the very definition of gallows humor.

No doubt about it, Heath was going to have to find a way to get that tin flask back to Ghede Brav sometime soon. The longer he held onto it, the more he felt as though the Lwa were all keeping an eye on him.

Having someone watch his back was one thing. Playing soap opera star for the Powers That Be was something different. Why were they paying so much attention to him anyway? Was it just the flask, or was it something more?

Just another question he didn't have the answer to. All the more reason he was looking forward to getting home and having a little time to himself.

Colin had offered to let Heath spend the night, but Heath wanted to get back inside his own wards. A place where his own little spirits were keeping an eye on him, and he might be able to consult the cards or the cowries in peace.

Not to mention the chance to restock a few of the things he kept in his backpack. Spend a little time with his cat. And most of all, he wanted to be bright-eyed and bushy-tailed when Goldilocks' limo showed up before the crack of dawn.

As though it were possible for Heath to be anything like bright-eyed and bushy-tailed at such an unholy hour.

So instead of crash space on Colin's couch, Heath accepted a lift home from Tony. Rather generous offer on the monk's part, since it was more than a little out of his way, and even more so because he refused gas money.

Tony drove an old Subaru Forester that looked as though it should have been animated and talking. But then, Heath felt that way about all the old Subarus. They just had this cartoonish shape through the early 2000s — longer than they should have been in places, and curved just right to have blinking eyes instead of headlights.

This particular Forester was powder blue, and freaking spotless. Even under the sodium lamps along the curb outside Colin's place, it gleamed enough that Heath must have gawked, because Tony laughed and explained that washing and polishing the car was part of the meditation practice of one of the younger monks.

Seems that particular monk was avid in his meditations.

The car's inside was just as spotless, and that was downright creepy. Gray cloth interior, and not a single sign of wear on the seats, the dashboard, anything. Only two things Heath could spot that convinced him the car hadn't been donated hours ago by some Subaru museum. First, it had a small, plastic statue of Saint Christopher on the dashboard in front of the steering wheel. Second, well, it smelled of frankincense. As though the monks held weekly mass in the backseat.

"Thank you for accepting a lift," Tony said, once the car was started and they were underway.

"Hey, you're the one doing me a favor, and I appreciate it."

"The ride is a small thing," Tony said, shaking his head, "and there's something I wanted to talk to you about. Colin's loyalty is admirable, but he is not Catholic. I'm not sure he would understand."

"I haven't been to mass in a long, long time. And don't even ask about confession."

"Nevertheless," Tony said, one finger thrust in the air for emphasis, "you were raised Catholic, and you have taken the Catechism. You're one of ours, whether you feel that way or not."

Those were almost exactly the same words Ghede Brav used to tell Heath his involvement with Vodou went deeper than he realized. And just as that thought occurred to him, Heath became aware that he could hear the faintest strains of Ghede Brav's smoky skulls saying, "Ding ding ding ding ding."

But Tony was still talking.

"...And for those reasons, and others, you will understand things Colin will not."

Heath opened his mouth to defend his friend, but decided Tony didn't mean any of this as an attack. So he closed his mouth again and let the monk continue.

"I believe Brother Theodopolis was right to assign me to assist you, even though, so far as I know, he does not know of my brother's involvement. Or, for that matter, that I even have a brother." He glanced at Heath, then back at the road. Tony was staying to the side streets for the drive to Heath's place, dark and quiet and few unparked cars. "We ... don't discuss the past much. Many who take the vows of our particular order have led ... troubled lives and feel more drawn to atonement than discussing their past sins."

"If this is a pitch to get me to vow up—"

"Oh, no," Tony said with a chuckle. "Nothing like that."

"Good, because even if I were curious — which I'm not — I could never handle the vows."

"My point is ... I'm troubled by this. By my involvement. And I was hoping you could help me understand."

"Not much more history between me and Drake than I've told you." Heath shrugged. "And for your piece, sounds simple enough. The Almighty doesn't want me laying too heavy a smack down on your brother. Or maybe He wants your brother to see the light. Or—"

"Only the Lord knows His plans for my brother." Tony shook his head. "No, I'm talking about my involvement. The Lord could have had sent any monk to assist you. Why me?"

Heath blinked. "'Cause we're talking about your brother? Seems pretty straightforward to me."

"That's just it," Tony said, and Heath could hear frustration in the monk's voice. "The Lord is noted for His mysterious ways. And I've learned from past experience, if I think I know His will, I'm missing something."

"So ... what, you think you need a reverse Occam's Razor to understand God?"

"Understanding the Lord is beyond any of us. The most we can hope to glean are fragments of His great plan. And this particular fragment—"

"I get it," Heath said with a chuckle. "The piece looks like it fits so neatly, you're just sure it belongs in a different jigsaw puzzle."

"Something like that."

"You want me to read for you? On the house."

"No," Tony said quickly. "The Bible proscribes divination in all its forms. While I would not chastise you for your practices — as you say, your soul knows its own fate better than I could claim to — that does not mean I'd be willing to—"

"What then?" Heath didn't try to keep the sigh out of his voice. "And keep in mind, if you continue coming down on the way I do things—"

"I meant no offense." Tony lingered for a moment at a stop sign near the end of Heath's block, so he could turn and look Heath in the eye. "Honest. If you wished to give confession, I would hear it, and grant you both absolution and communion when you finished. But it is not my place to tell anyone how to live and work, least of all someone who has proven himself an ally to our cause."

"All right, all right," Heath said, waving a hand. "If you're not asking me for that, just what exactly are you asking for?"

"The nature of your work makes you ... observant ... in ways that others are not. Now that you understand the nature of my question, it may be that sometime, during the course of our work together, you may receive a flash of insight about why, exactly, the Lord has chosen me for this particular duty."

Apparently they'd lingered too long at that stop sign. Behind them, a motorcycle honked what was supposed to pass for a horn. Sounded more to Heath like a roadrunner with a sore throat. But the sound made Tony jump, and get the car moving again.

"Is that all?" Heath asked, as the motorcycle roared around the Subaru, while Tony pulled up to the curb outside Heath's place. "Sure. 'Course. Gotta warn you though. These sorts of revelations, they tend to come after the fact."

"Or at the moment of greatest trial." Tony grimaced. "If such is His will, then that's how it will go. I admit though, I was hoping for a little advanced warning."

Heath chuckled and shook the monk's hand before getting out of the car. He waved goodbye as Tony drove away, then whistled to himself as he wandered down the driveway toward the backyard and his cottage.

That was the most roundabout way anyone had ever asked Heath for a divination. So roundabout the monk might even have fooled himself...

5

No good night's sleep ever ended before dawn. In fact, as far as Heath was concerned, no good night's sleep ever ended before noon.

And the idea of deliberately arising during a so-called morning hour whose name began with an "f?" Well, Heath could think of a good word for that idea that also began with an "f."

In other words, Heath felt as though his head had only barely had time to dent his big, soft pillow before his alarm started blaring the auditory equivalent of diarrhea.

But a deal was a deal, and a payday was a payday. So, some fifteen minutes before dawn on Friday morning, Heath found himself not only wide awake and dressed, but once again in a rear leather bucket seat of the big, black, Mercedes S-class car driven by Hershel.

Heath was wearing a dark-blue-and-white striped button-up shirt, with short sleeves, and cargo shorts the same shade of dark blue. He had on a pork pie hat, also dark blue, and he wore his boat shoes without socks. And, of course, his backpack sat on the floorboards between his knees, fully stocked and ready for whatever the day held.

Or so he hoped.

He'd fortified himself for the meeting with a pair of hardboiled eggs and two slices of wheat toast with orange marmalade, along with a strong cup of black coffee. He had the feeling that it wouldn't be enough.

Hershel was in the same kind of suit as yesterday. Might even have been the same exact suit, but if so at least it didn't smell slept-in. Only smell in the car, apart from the leather, was a hint of Goldilocks' honeysuckle.

Hershel had yet to speak a word in Heath's presence. Might even have been mute, for all Heath could tell. Not that it mattered much. In Heath's experience, very few big men with buzz cuts had anything nice to say to him. Even the middle-aged ones, wearing suits.

So Heath was content to ease back in his seat and try to ignore the movement of the car.

And if the driver-slash-bodyguard decided that Heath fell asleep, maybe he'd let something slip. Make a call he shouldn't have made or something.

At least Heath already had his money. Goldilocks had taken the in-advance part of their relationship seriously, and Hershel had handed over a crisp white envelope full of crisp green bills before even opening the car door for Heath. Didn't even seem to mind Heath counting it right there in front of him.

No scents, no oils, no dusts, no juju, nothing. Nice, safe money. Heath's favorite kind, and — despite Nariko's admonitions — in a quantity sufficient to make him feel a *little* better about the obscenely early hour.

Hershel didn't make any phone calls during the drive. Didn't play with the radio either. Didn't do anything except drive the car. So either he didn't believe Heath had fallen asleep, or Hershel was just that boring.

Well, either that, or Hershel was actually an automaton. Golem, maybe, what with the Jewish name and all. Big enough, and mute…

Nah. Goldilocks came across about as Jewish as Heath was a Muslim. And while he didn't know much about golems, he had the distinct impression they were only for the faithful.

Heath'd *just* gotten to the point of speculating what else Hershel might be when Hershel did the most interesting thing he'd done so far.

He spoke.

His tone was smoother than Heath expected, and almost as gentle as Tony's.

"You having us followed, Mr. Cyr? I don't advise it."

"I told exactly three people that I have a meeting at sunup. One of them is out of the country, and the other two expressed commiseration about the early hour. None of them offered to follow me or try to keep me safe."

"So you don't know anybody in a powder blue Subaru Forester? An oh-three?"

"Well..."

"Mr. Cyr, if you know that person, believe me when I say you want to tell me. I doubt ... Goldilocks told you not to have anyone following you, so I'm inclined to let one instance go. But if that person isn't a friend of yours, something very bad is about to happen to them."

"I know a guy with a powder blue Subaru Forester. Don't know the year."

Heath turned and looked back to see Tony following them, maybe three cars back and not making eye contact.

"That him?" Hershel asked.

"Yes." Heath pulled out his phone and held it up. Hershel nodded. Heath dialed the mobile number Tony gave him last night. Watched Tony answer hands-free.

"Good morning, Heath. I trust you slept well. Or, at least, as well as you could, given your night-owlish tendencies."

"Yeah. Well enough. Tony, you need to not follow us."

"It rarely hurts to let those of questionable intention know that you have allies."

"They know. Believe me. But they also have a problem with being followed."

"And I have no doubt that the Lord will protect me from any evil they wish to perpetrate."

"Tony, I'm trying to *cut down* on the number of people trying to kill me. This is not helping."

"You think you're kidding," Hershel said, loudly enough that Heath was pretty sure those words were meant for Tony, "but you're not. This is a delicate situation, and you don't want Goldilocks thinking you don't trust her. And you definitely don't want me to start feeling uncomfortable."

Big words for a man who, as far as Heath could tell, packed no mojo of his own. But then, plenty of ways to kill a man that didn't involve magic...

"You heard?" Heath asked Tony.

"I heard. Sad are those who meet precaution with threats." Tony sighed. "Very well. Let your driver know that your ride home will be tended to, and in the meantime I'll pick up coffee and donuts."

"Thank you," Heath said, as much surprise in his own voice as relief.

After Heath put the phone away, Hershel nodded at Heath in the mirror.

"Thanks," Hershel said. "Wouldn't be the first priest I've killed, but between the two of us, I don't like doing it. I may not agree with them about religion, but I don't like killing any man of faith. Or woman, for that matter."

While he wasn't going to correct Hershel, Heath wasn't sure Tony was a priest. In his recollection, every priest went by the title "Father," and a monk who went by the title "Brother" was no priest. Still, Tony acted like a priest, and he *had* offered to hear Heath's confession...

Then a different question made its way through Heath's sleepy mind.

"Does 'man of faith' include me?"

"Yep," Hershel said, pulling the car into the same underground garage as yesterday. "Killing you would be strictly business. But I'd feel bad about it later."

Heath locked eyes with Hershel in the mirror. Held the look between them. Not enough to start the *compelling gaze*, but enough to let a few hints of his own power slip on through to make a point.

"How would you do it?" he asked.

"You?" Hershel cocked his head slightly to the side. "I'll spare you the details, but I have yet to run across a ward that can stop a big enough explosion."

"That a fact." Heath was impressed by how *un*impressed he managed to sound.

"Yep. Learned to blow things up back in the teams. Always was good at it. And when you're good at something, there's always money to be made doing it."

"Bit risky telling me this, isn't it?" Heath asked, voice still level. "Guys like me are very good at contingencies."

"Hey." Hershel smiled. "I'm not issuing a threat here. You asked if I'd like killing you. Wouldn't. You're a man of faith. Plus, figure you for the straight-shooter type. Shame to kill a straight-shooter, and worse when he's a man of faith. But if I had to, believe me when I tell you I could."

"That may be," Heath said, "but you might not survive doing it."

Hershel shrugged. If he was bluffing, Heath couldn't tell.

"The guy in the Surbaru's going to pick me up."

Hershel chuckled, and Heath got out of the car. Across the lot he could see the elevator from yesterday, standing open and waiting for him. Like a mouth, waiting to swallow him whole.

Maybe Nariko was right. Maybe Heath wasn't getting paid enough for this gig after all.

***

GOLDILOCKS WASN'T WAITING IN AN OFFICE THIS TIME. SHE'D STAKED out a small conference room. Or at least, the sign on the door identified Conference Room A as "Small Conference Room A." Which did make Heath wonder if there was a "Large Conference Room A," and perhaps an "Enormous Conference Room A," complete with arena-style seating.

Because if *this* conference room was "small," Heath wanted to know just how big this firm's meetings got.

The slate gray table down the center of "Small Conference Room A" could seat a dozen people, and the walls had two huge flat-screen televisions on swivel mounts, one at each end. One long wall was all white boards, with dry erase markers in a rainbow of colors, and the other wall was all windows (currently tucked away behind closed blinds).

Twelve big, black leather chairs sat around that table, waiting for the Illuminati or something. This whole office building just had the feel of conspiracies and the kind of people who probably ran the world from behind closed doors.

Speaking of which.

Goldilocks was dressed for ... well ... magic or seduction, and Heath devoutly hoped it was magic. She stood at one end of the room, wearing a short silk robe, black, with esoteric symbols embroidered in gold thread. The robe barely fell to her knees and showed off her admittedly shapely calves. Her long blond hair was tied back in a ponytail, and if she wore a drop of makeup, Heath couldn't tell.

He smelled dragon's blood, which meant she'd already burned incense and put her censer away. Unless she was using it for perfume...

Could this woman really be that strange?

"I hope you're not wearing that on my account," Heath said, twitching his finger at the robe as he slung his backpack down at the far end of the table from her.

"I am, as it happens." Goldilocks posed with her fists on her hips. "I work naked, as the gods intended. However, in my experience, the sight of a well-formed naked woman destroys most men's ability to concentrate on anything but the sight of her flesh."

She arched an eyebrow. "Or do you declare yourself an exception to this rule?"

"Whether I am or not, by all means, keep your robe on." Heath plopped down in the chair next to his backpack, making the leather seat hiss out its air. "Wouldn't want you to think I was here for anything other than perfectly professional reasons. And my professional services do not extend to anything that would make either of us get naked."

"Good to know." She reached down to the carpet for an Armani suitcase and set it on top of the table. She started to unzip it, but Heath cleared his throat noisily. She blinked up at him, evidently unaware that, bent over as she was, she was on the verge of spilling out of her robe.

Heath told her so with a gesture, which made her smirk as she tightened her robe closed.

"Just want to point out," Heath said, "that you aren't likely to need anything you keep in that case during our meeting. Unless you'd like me to step out of the room for a moment while you put on some actual clothes."

"I have ritual equipment in here."

"Including dragon's blood incense, I know. But you won't be casting anything while I'm here with you. That was never part of our arrangement."

"You are to consult with me about my Vizinha problem. Your presence during the casting of important spells was implied."

"It most certainly was not." Heath put his feet up on the table. "I'm here to talk strategies and approaches. I believe I told you I'd be happy to take your money and tell you all the places you're going wrong. I said nothing at all about watching you work."

"How will you tell me where I'm going wrong if you don't watch the process itself?"

Heath shook his head. "Planning. Not execution. Participating in the execution phase would be as bad as going after Vizinha myself, which, as I told you, is not on the table as an option."

"I'm not getting much service for my money then."

"You're not paying all that much, either. You're paying enough for me to listen to your plans and tell you why they won't work. Maybe even enough for me to suggest a few options that might. But not nearly enough to get me to do so much as dress a candle for you."

That got Heath a raised eyebrow and a pair of crossed arms. The way this woman loved to pose, Heath was betting she'd tried to become a model. Took all the right classes for posture and posing, but failed at being anorexic.

Heath, however, felt no need to answer a raised eyebrow. Especially not when he was irritated at yet another customer trying to get more out of him than they were paying for.

"Very well," Goldilocks said with a sigh. "I'll ask. What does dressing a candle mean?"

Heath laughed hard enough he had to slap his thigh, which darkened the look in those blue eyes of hers. Not that he felt over-concerned, despite the not-inconsiderable aura of power she no longer hid.

"Prepping a spell into a candle for a client. Client burns the candle, and as it burns the spell works. By the time it's burnt away, they've got what they were after."

Goldilocks tapped her chin with a long finger.

"Just what could you do with a dressed candle?"

"For you?" Heath shook his head. "Nothing. Not while you're fighting with Vizinha. Professional courtesy."

"Oh, enough!"

Goldilocks strode toward Heath fast enough that he yanked his feet down off the table and jammed one hand into his backpack. But instead of threatening him, she rolled out the chair next to him and perched on the edge of the seat.

"Fine then," she said, one eyebrow judgmentally high. "You're being paid for your advice. Advise me. How would you go about trying to kill Vizinha?"

"Wrong question," Heath said, pulling his hand out of his backpack. "Doesn't matter how I'd try to do it. I'm not you. You work differently than I do."

"I'm not talking about magic now. I'm talking about strategy."

Goldilocks' tone and posture were all business, but something to her aspect was off. She had an air of ... angry sexuality to her. And her pupils were dilated more than they should have been, bright as the conference room lights were.

And there was something more. Something Heath couldn't put a finger on.

He was starting to get the feeling he wasn't here to be a consultant...

"All right," Heath said, standing up as much to put a little distance between himself and Goldilocks as to let him approach the white board. And he brought his backpack with him. "This is Vizinha."

Heath drew an X on the board with whatever marker he picked up first. Purple, as it happened. He drew three circles around the X, then a series of smaller circles enclosing those.

"These are her casual defenses." He tapped the small circles. "Helper spirits." Next he tapped the three circles around the X. "Wards. On her. On her places. And the blessings of her patron *Orixás*."

"Looks pretty thorough," Goldilocks said.

"And these are just her casual defenses. What she keeps in place at all times, because the woman has plenty of enemies. More than I do, if you can believe it. If she thinks you're after her — or she thinks anyone else is coming after her — you can add another circle or two. Maybe thicken up all the circles." Heath shrugged. "Depends on how you want to picture it."

"So how do I get at someone like Vizinha?"

The question was casual. Just the right kind of casual. It matched everything Heath knew about Goldilocks. Her style, her intonation. Everything about those words sounded perfectly innocent and natural, in and of themselves.

Well, as innocent and natural as anyone *could* sound, given that they were talking about homicide.

But when Goldilocks asked those words, all the little hairs on Heath's arms and on the back of his neck, every one of them stood at attention. And he got that sudden feeling of being watched.

He turned and looked at Goldilocks straight on. Didn't open his spirit eyes, just trusted his experience to notice anything he needed to notice.

Nothing. He couldn't spot anything off about her. She just looked like any one of the countless people born lucky enough not to have even a touch of magic about them.

But that was just it. She looked *too normal* for a practitioner. She didn't even look like she had a touch of undeveloped power, which is how most *good* practitioners looked when they bothered hiding what they were. After all, get on a crowded elevator and probably a third of the people on it have a touch of undeveloped talent.

But this woman looked devoid of anything that wasn't completely normal.

She was alone in a warded room — wards that she admitted to casting — with another practitioner, and she still looked magically tone deaf.

That meant she was either the biggest, baddest practitioner Heath had ever run across, or something else entirely.

"You're good," he said. "I almost missed it. Almost. But, honey, there's nobody more subtle than my uncle, and I've been dealing with his crap longer than you'd believe. And I'm still here."

"I'm not sure what you mean, Mr. Cyr." Wary eyes and wary posture, but Goldilocks wasn't giving up the game yet.

"Deal's canceled," he said, slinging the backpack over one shoulder while keeping his left hand near a certain packet of powders in a pocket of his shorts. "You've been lying to me about the whole thing, so I'm keeping all payments to date. What with you operating in bad faith, and all."

"Wait!" Goldilocks said, both hands coming up like Heath had pulled a gun on her. But there was something more honest in her eyes now than Heath had seen so far. But whether it was fear or something else, he couldn't be sure.

Heath slipped that left hand into his pocket, in case this was a bluff.

"Don't cancel our deal, Mr. Cyr. Please." Her hands came down, folded in her lap. "Vizinha needs to die. It's the only way."

"Look," Heath said. "I don't like cryptic shit at the best of times, and it's way too goddamn early to expect me to be patient about it now. Tell me what the hell is going on here — really going on — or I walk."

Goldilocks sighed. Not exasperated or impatient, but this deep, heartfelt sound of longing and loss.

Something shifted inside her. No. Not quite inside her. But not quite behind her either. Heath itched to open his spirit eyes, but got the feeling in his gut that it would be a bad idea. Even his normal eyesight told Heath that Goldilocks had put on a false face. And she'd done it well enough that he'd almost missed it.

"Please, Mr. Cyr." Goldilocks gestured to the chair Heath had occupied earlier. "You have asked for honesty, and that is not a simple thing for such as me. But in this case, I think it must be necessary."

Goldilocks' voice had changed. Gained a depth it hadn't had before, as well as a ... sweetness.

Damballah, Heath muttered too soft for anyone but the Lwa to hear. If they were going to watch him, the least they could do was help out. *Protect me please.*

But Heath took that chair.

And Goldilocks began to change right before his eyes.

WHEN HEATH HAD MET GOLDILOCKS, SHE'D LOOKED LIKE THE KIND OF generic beauty that he could have seen in television dramas or on network news. Perfect hair, perfect teeth, symmetrical features and the right kind of curves and skin to make Middle America stiffen up below the waist.

But there in "Small" Conference Room A, Goldilocks' whole form shifted. Now she had Creole café au lait skin and a frizz of reddish brown hair, but bright green eyes. Her curves slimmed a bit, but stayed pleasantly present under that robe.

And all of this was perfectly visible to his normal eyes. Which told Heath that what his spirit eyes would have seen would have been more than he wanted to deal with at this hour. He had the sneaking suspicion that this Creole look both was and was not her real form. It was honest where the blond look had been a lie, but it wasn't quite the whole truth either.

Still, Heath's heart rate sped more than he would have liked to admit. Definitely the kind of detail to omit when he eventually told Nariko about this meeting. Much like the details that his mouth was suddenly dry, and he could feel sweat on his palms.

He had to clear his throat before he could speak.

"I said I wanted the truth." Heath gestured up and down as though her whole appearance were just a suit of clothes, which he figured had to be close to the truth. "That's not really you either, is it?"

"No," Goldilocks said, and though the moniker didn't quite fit anymore, Heath persisted with it in his head. Didn't matter how she looked, only that he associated the name with the ... person?

She quirked a half-smile. "This is, though, about as close as I can come in your presence. If you were homosexual, perhaps, I could do better. If you were asexual, I could do better yet. But you aren't either of those, so..."

She spread her arms helplessly, as though her glorious appearance were his ... fault...

"What *are* you?" Heath said, awe in his voice.

"I am what men want Scarlett Johannson to be. What they wanted Marilyn Monroe to be. I am the fantasy of the centerfold, of the Victoria's Secret catalog, of the letter to *Penthouse*. When American men dream of sex, they dream of me, and when they pleasure themselves their climaxes are my offerings."

Heath scratched at the tip of his chin with one finger.

"That's as direct as you can say it, isn't it?"

Goldilocks nodded.

"Just when I think nothing more can surprise me." Heath shook his head. "I once heard Maggie's grandmother lament that this land doesn't have ... good neighbors, the way her native Ireland does. A few expatriates, but that's it. She complained that Americans have been buil— finding their own." No need to get insulting. "She was talking about folks like you, wasn't she? Because the Europeans who moved here, they couldn't connect with the native spirits of this land the way they had back home."

"Precisely," Goldilocks said. "The stories changed here, and instead of making the land more welcoming for the *sidhe* and the *wights*, the new American dreams and ideals began to form, well, me. And others like me."

"But when my folk were brought here, ours came with us."

"Yes and no." She tilted her head in thought in a way that showed off her graceful neck. "Your gods and intermediaries came with you, same as theirs did, but your local spirits stayed in Africa. Still, your people had an easier time connecting with the local spirits."

Heath was all ready to make a comment about the different "relationship" the former Europeans had with the natives, as compared to the former Africans, but her "others like me" comment rang in his head.

"Wait. So Liberty's a tall green lady?"

"To some. To others she is an eagle. Still others, a serpent."

"And Hershel. He's one of you, isn't he?"

"He is the Bodyguard, and he's watching over me in this troubled time." She sighed. "I only wish he could assault Vizinha, but attacking—"

"Is outside his province." Heath nodded, then frowned. "Isn't there an idealized American soldier who could—"

"The Soldier battles political enemies, not personal."

"Assassin, perhaps?"

Goldilocks puckered her lips in thought.

"There's the Mobster. But the price of his help is almost always worse than whatever problem he solves."

Heath chuckled at that, then realized something.

"Hang on a second. If you're the American ideal of sex, why would you look more like ... whatever you normally look like ... if I were gay? Wouldn't you just be a hot guy?"

"No," she said with a shake of her head, and Heath had to fight not to watch that frizz of red hair bounce enticingly. "I could not be all things to all people. I am one half of the perfect couple."

"Let me guess. Your counterpart sprang forth fully formed from dreams of romance novels and Chippendale dancers?"

"Something like that. He tells it better than I do."

A wave of cold realization washed over Heath. He closed his eyes. He didn't want to say what occurred to him. Didn't want to ask the question he had to ask. The question he already knew the answer to.

"Why couldn't I have just stormed out?" he muttered. "Why? When am I going to learn? Knowing too much is what's going to get me killed one day."

"Mr. Cyr?" Something that sounded like honest concern in Goldilocks' voice. Or at least, as honest as she was capable of being, all things considered. "Is something wrong?"

"This perfect man. This other half of the perfect couple. He's the problem. Isn't he?"

Goldilocks nodded. She looked about to speak, but Heath beat her to it.

"Let me guess. Vizinha has captured him. Either for her own lascivious purposes, or for her magic."

"Both," Goldilocks said in a flat tone. "He and I are not meant to be bound. To be used. She will destroy him if I do not free him."

Heath grimaced, but had to ask. "Won't he just re-form?"

"He might. But it would take untold time. Such as we do not form overnight. And without him, heterosexual women will suffer. Homosexual men will suffer. He and I, we don't merely receive and encapsulate, we inspire and enflame. Without one of us, without our perfected copulation, the imbalance could be dreadful. Artists without their muses, couples growing cold. Fights, and worse. And as his absence stretched, tensions would grow. Violence. Rape. Murder."

"Mass hysteria. I get it." Heath sighed. "Looks like I'm squaring off against Vizinha again after all. Damn it."

"Truly, Mr. Cyr? You will help me, even knowing what must be done?"

"I'll help. But we've got to renegotiate. You aren't paying me *near* enough for this gig."

HEATH HAD HALF-HOPED THAT TAKING A HARD NEGOTIATING STANCE would have given him the chance to walk away from this. Yes, the consequences sounded dire, and yes, his conscience might not have let him in any event. But the fantasy was lovely.

Then he would have only had to worry about *one* person trying to kill him at the moment.

His life was definitely going the wrong direction.

Unfortunately, Goldilocks had been only too happy to meet his demands regarding salary, expenses, and even a bonus if he actually pulled this off. Plus, she was still willing to help, and if she was even a third as big a deal as she made herself sound, she was a resource not to be discounted.

By the time Heath was ready to leave Small Conference Room A, another half-hour later, he had a pretty good idea of what had happened, and how, even if he didn't yet know what he was going to do about it.

And just before he left, Heath turned back to Goldilocks and said, "One thing's been bugging me. If you don't mind."

"You can ask me anything, Mr. Cyr," she said with a devastating smile that got his stomach fluttering.

"Should I ... should I be worried that you don't look Japanese to me?"

Goldilocks laughed, and it was the kind of rich sound that could have surrounded Heath and made him feel all warm and safe. If he let it.

"Let me answer that by asking you a question." She raised one reddish eyebrow. "Mr. Cyr, you've been in my presence for the better part of an hour, and most of that has been with me looking just the way I do in dreams so deep you might not even remember them."

She leaned forward, letting her robe bow just a little. "This is the look of your dream girl, Mr. Cyr. And yet, have you found yourself ... standing at attention? Even once?"

Heath shook his head.

"Of course not. I'm just a fantasy. You're a man in love, Mr. Cyr. And what fantasy can compare to the real thing?"

Something unknotted in Heath's gut.

"Half the reason I came to you was your experience with Vizinha. But the other half was your palpable love for Nariko Tachibana. I couldn't seduce you if I tried, which makes you the perfect person to help me."

"You're sure?" Heath shook his head quickly. "I mean, I'm pretty sure I know how I feel about Nariko, but I'd hate to find out the hard way that—"

"Mr. Cyr, did it even *occur* to you to include a night with me in the asking price for your help?"

"Of course not."

"Of course not. I'm over a barrel. I need you. I would have said yes and not thought twice about it. But it didn't even occur to you to ask."

"Thank you," Heath said with a small smile.

"No, Mr. Cyr. Thank *you.*"

6

TONY WAS WAITING AT THE CURB WHEN HEATH LEFT THE PARKING LOT. He'd gone out the way he came in, but didn't even spare Hershel a glance as he walked toward the street. He'd been too tempted to make some kind of a bodyguard crack, movie reference maybe, and that wouldn't have helped anyone.

The passenger door of Tony's Subaru was already open, and Tony held a steaming to-go cup of Stumptown Coffee toward Heath. Heath hummed with pleasure at the rich, roasted smell as he eased himself into his seat.

"Donuts in the backseat," Tony said, "but I'll have a hard time pulling away from the curb if you don't close the door and put on your seatbelt."

"Sorry," Heath said, still reveling in the scent of the coffee. Smelled like Nariko's kitchen. Must have been the same blend of beans she bought.

Two hours. His video call with her was only about two hours away. On the one hand, Heath couldn't wait to see her, to talk to her. On the other, he knew she was going to be pissed about what he'd just agreed to. Even if she might — *might* — agree that he charged enough.

Tony cleared his throat loudly.

"Right." Heath closed the car door and strapped on his seat belt before allowing himself his first sip of the coffee. Yep. Just like Nariko's.

Tony pulled away from the curb and eased into the morning downtown traffic, heading for the Burnside Bridge to head back to the west side. Light traffic right now, as it would likely remain until close to the lunch hour. White clouds instead of gray overhead providing a reminder that this was still the Portland summertime. As though the heat left any doubt. Already in the seventies, and building.

"So," Tony said after a couple of blocks, in a poor attempt at an offhand fashion. "How did your meeting go?"

"I didn't help her kill anyone, if that's what you're asking."

"Good. Good."

"Instead I agreed to do it."

Tony braked hard enough to slam Heath against his seatbelt and slosh hot coffee down to burn his lap. A horn blared behind them.

"Ow!" Heath said.

"You *what*?" Tony had the kind of righteous fury in his eyes that Heath always imagined went with the Inquisition.

"I'm kidding, I'm kidding," Heath said, patting at the coffee on his shorts with paper napkins from the Foresters' center console. "Drive already."

Heath waited until they were on the bridge before clarifying, making a show out of drying his shorts and sipping his coffee down to levels that shouldn't spill out of the travel lid. Meanwhile, Tony was tense enough to make the air in the car feel thick.

"I didn't agree to kill anybody," Heath said.

"Just what *did* you agree to?"

No braking. No looking away from the road. Heath figured it was as safe to answer that question as it was likely to get.

"I agreed to help free the American embodiment of the perfect man from Vizinha's evil clutches."

Tony furrowed his brow, but didn't say anything until they were off the bridge. Heath might have found that encouraging, if the air in the car felt any less tense. So he sipped a little more coffee, then rooted around in the back for a donut.

Heath had just found a chocolate glazed when Tony spoke again.

"That wasn't a joke, was it? I have trouble telling with you."

"Nope," Heath said around a tasty bite of chocolate donut. He did Tony the courtesy of swallowing before he explained. And Tony did Heath the courtesy of not saying anything further until Heath was finished explaining.

"Is there a saint?"

That was Tony's first question. Of all the potential questions he could have asked, *that* was the one he settled on?

"Can't say it occurred to me to ask," Heath said, returning to his donut.

"Religion has been an important part of American life since before its founding. I imagine there must be. But if there is, what does that mean? And if there isn't—"

"Tony?" Heath resisted the urge to reach out and shake Tony's shoulder, but only barely. "You're going the wrong way. This is back toward—"

"Colin's house, I know." Tony smiled. "We're having breakfast with him before your call with Nariko."

Heath blasted out a breath through his nose.

"Really? And have the two of you decided on my afternoon schedule yet?"

"No," Tony said, his tone light, "we thought we'd play that by ear."

Heath eased back in his seat and grumbled, "That's it. I've got to start driving for myself more often."

MAYBE TEN MINUTES LATER HEATH WAS SEATED AT COLIN'S KITCHEN table, across from Colin and Tony. Colin was wearing cutoff jean shorts with a sleeveless Metallica *Kill 'Em All* tee shirt. Tony was still wearing all black.

Both of them look too damned chipper for an hour of the morning that Heath would rather have slept through.

The three of them were still working through Tony's huge box of donuts, but they were drinking Colin's coffee now. Too much hazelnut, especially to drink with donuts, but the caffeine was more than welcome in Heath's system. And the perking of Colin's coffee maker made for a cheerful backdrop to their conversation.

Heath had said nothing while Tony did an admirably accurate job of bringing Colin up to speed. When he finished, Colin looked at Heath and shook his head.

"Nariko's gonna *kill* you."

"Why am I here?" Heath held up a halting hand. "Don't get me wrong, Colin. I love you like a brother, and I'm going to need you and Tony to help me through this mess. But why am I here, acting like this is a normal time of day to be awake and active, instead of back in my comfy bed, snoozing away the morning hours until Nariko calls?"

"We didn't schedule that meeting for you," Tony said.

"But," Colin added, "we had the feeling you'd need to talk to us when it was over."

"Okay," Heath said, "if the two of you start doing the horror-movie-twin thing and speaking in unison, I'm out of here."

Colin snickered, once more reminding Heath of a cartoon dog.

"It's my fault," Tony said. "I could not sit idle while you had your meeting. I called Colin and convinced him you would need a strategy session afterwards."

"Given what happened at your meeting," Colin said with a smile. "I think he's right."

"The question is," Tony said, "which strategies should we plan first? Your battle with my brother, or your rescue of ... what did you call him, Colin?"

"Mr. Perfect." Colin smiled. "And I want to be there when we rescue him."

"Of course you do," Heath said. Then sighed. Then sipped his coffee and shook his head. "I'm going to have to go after Drake first. He's already taken a shot at me, and he's announced when his big guns are coming online. I need to hit him first."

"That doesn't leave me much time to find a nonviolent answer."

"Go talk to him now, if you like." Heath raised a finger to make his point. "But not as my emissary. You go, you're not representing me in any way. You're just his brother, trying to save his life. Or his soul." Heath shrugged. "Hell. Both. I don't care."

"What if he presents himself as a mediator?" Colin asked.

"Nope," Heath said with a slow, firm shake of his head. "He's already spoken to me. If Tony presents himself as a mediator, it will look like I asked for mediation. Or at least, Drake will be able to spin it that way."

Tony looked as though he were going to object, but Heath cut in ahead of him.

"Remember, this community is my client base. I do have to care what they think."

"That makes my position tenuous at best."

"How do you think I feel? I need this solved, quick and decisive."

Then a truly evil idea occurred to Heath. Bad enough to make him smile a smile that made Colin shudder just to see.

"He has an idea," Colin said softly, "but I'm not sure we want to hear it."

Heath let that smile stretch wide. Then shuddered as he realized how much he must have resembled his uncle in that moment.

The smile vanished. The pleasure leading to the smile vanished with it. But the idea remained, and it still might have been worth doing.

"Tell him I'm not going to stop with his death," Heath said.

"What do you mean?" Tony asked, and from his tone Heath thought Tony might have an idea of exactly what Heath meant. He just didn't want to believe it.

"I mean there are ways to trap the soul after death and make it serve me. Baron Samedi would be only too happy to teach me how it's done. Hell, my uncle would fly in just to show me the ropes." Heath met the monk's brown eyes. "Drake wants to make a public example of me? I'll make an example out of *him*."

Heath leaned forward and continued. Even the coffee maker seemed to still as he spoke.

"I'll make his dead body dance on tables at Gripper. I'll send his soul into the dreams of my enemies. *No one* will mess with me when I'm through with him."

Tony crossed himself and muttered a quick prayer in Latin. Colin didn't move a muscle.

"Are you serious, Heath?" Tony asked.

"You tell me," Heath said, holding on to that same intensity. "No prayers. No angels forcing my hand. You look into my eyes and tell me if I'm serious."

The monk did just that.

"I..." Tony shook his head. Crossed himself again. "In the name of the Father, the Son, and the Holy Spirit I believe you are."

"Then if you have any love for your brother. If you don't want to see his soul become my plaything before it goes to its final judgment, then you better go talk your brother into publicly rescinding that challenge and apologizing. Otherwise I'm going to end this once and for all."

Tony didn't stay to finish his coffee. He stood straightaway and headed for the door, without even pausing to say goodbye.

Once the front door was closed behind him, and Heath could hear that Forester start up and peel out, only then did he sag back into his chair with a sigh.

"Holy shit," Colin said, disbelief all over his face. "Were you bluffing?"

Heath winked. "I was raised Catholic. Think that's the first time I ever lied to a priest?"

Colin's jaw dropped.

"Remind me never to play poker with you."

"Poker?" Heath smiled. "Been meaning to learn that game. Sure you don't want to teach me? Maybe with four or five rich friends?"

Colin snickered.

HEATH CAUGHT A RIDE HOME FROM COLIN JUST A LITTLE WHILE LATER. Colin had been making noises about planning strategies as they finished their breakfast, but he kept interrupting the process to speculate about Ms. Perfect and Mr. Perfect, as Colin insisted on calling Goldilocks and her other half. Wondering how each would look to him. What a threesome with them would be like.

It was when he'd finally wondered aloud what Mr. Perfect would look like to Nariko that Heath called a halt to the conversation and asked for the ride home.

On the ride home, Colin speculated aloud about whether or not Vizinha was banging Mr. Perfect, and what that might do to how she looked at other men afterwards.

By that point, Heath just tipped his pork pie hat forward until the brim covered his eyes, and pretended to sleep.

Finally, Colin was gone, and Heath was alone on his own front porch. No spirits waiting in the air except a handful of locals who kept an eye on the place for Heath. In the yard around him, the birds and squirrels kept up what Heath assumed was their normal morning chatter.

Not even any death threats tacked to his white front door. Just the black, equal-armed cross he'd painted himself, along with the key below it. His personal tribute to Papa Legba.

But a painted key didn't open doors, so Heath pulled his own keys from the pocket of his cargo shorts and let himself into his cottage apartment.

Home.

The place had been built as an in-law apartment, or an au pair unit. Heath could never decide which, but he leaned toward in-law apartment. Too much trouble and expense to go to for an au pair.

Had a big living room, and a big, roomy kitchen with lots of natural light from huge windows and skylights. One full bath and one half-bath, and a good-sized bedroom with a walk-in closet. Hardwood floors that could be heated in the wintertime.

When Heath had moved in, the place had been painted polar bear white to maximize the natural light. That had lasted two months before Heath painted the walls a muted pale green he found easier on the eyes.

Right now two dozen herbs hung from the living room ceiling to dry, filling the air with the kind of relaxing smell that made Heath smile. Taking up the path of conjure had taught him many things he wished he didn't know, and forced him to deal with people he'd rather not know existed. Like Drake, and the demons who served him.

But there was a simple tactile joy to preparing herbs and oils that Heath found both soothing and meditative.

Directly underneath those hanging herbs rested the solid oak work bench where Heath did most of that grinding, blending and mixing. Three different mortars and pestles, along with every tool he ever needed to grind, shred, chop, mix, stir or whatever. A stack of Sterno cans off to one side, for the things he needed to heat.

The work bench stood at the perfect height for Heath to do prep work while he sat in his main indulgence — a deep leather recliner that heated, massaged, and probably did even more if Heath ever got around to reading the instructions.

Along the walls of the living room and kitchen were landscapes that Heath found evocative. World famous juke joint Tipatina's, as seen from the street. The French Quarter in New Orleans. Haiti from the sea. The Saut d'Eau Waterfalls.

A couple of walnut bookcases housed his personal notebooks, as well as his reference books and materials. Not much that could have been bought in a store. Most of them were handwritten, but a few others had been printed in small batches on cheap paper as part of a knowledge exchange program among conjure workers back in the 70s, before Heath was even born.

Standing out like a weed among roses was the wall-mounted, fifty-inch flat screen television Colin had insisted on buying and installing. Truth was, Heath was just as happy to listen to music in the evenings, but Colin had known Heath maybe a month when he insisted that Heath keep up with pop culture.

Colin did have a point. Heath found the knowledge useful in dealing with clients. And modern shows were more entertaining than he remembered from his childhood.

A leather loveseat sat before the television, purchased after Nariko's first night at Heath's place.

His blond pressboard kitchen table had two chairs now for the same reason. The cabinets were white oak, and the matching sea green dishware and elegant, bottom-heavy glasses were gifts from Nariko, who hated his old mismatched, Thrift store surplus collection.

The mugs she left alone. Heath had an array of bizarre mugs that she actually approved of, which Heath had taken as a good sign in the early days of their dating. Before they'd broken up for the first time.

They'd broken up and gotten back together three times now — or was it four? It couldn't have been four — which made Heath wonder about what Goldilocks had been saying about Heath being "completely in love."

Did this mean they were fated to keep breaking up and getting back together? Not a fun thought.

Heath hauled himself through to the bedroom, where his tuxedo cat Dr. John was still stretched out, white furry belly exposed to the world, on the unmade sheets of his king-size bed.

That bed wasn't a concession to anybody. The day Heath had moved in, he measured how much space he'd need for his psychedelically painted bureau and his twin octagonal nightstands. When he realized he had enough room for a California king it was his first purchase.

Dr. John *murred* a sleepy complaint that the hour was too damned early for Heath to be making all that racket, and that Heath had no business being out of bed in the first place.

Or at least, that was what Heath figured the cat was saying. Two years old and already smarter than his owner.

Heath dropped down onto the bed next to his cat and fell fast asleep.

HEATH WAS DRAGGED BACK TO CONSCIOUSNESS BY A TRILLING BEEPING noise. By the time he blinked sleep out of his eyes, he was sitting up. Light streamed in through his bedroom windows, dappled by the Douglas firs outside.

His bedroom. On his bed. That was good.

Fully dressed. Dark blue and white striped shirt, dark blue cargo shorts. Brown leather boat shoes still on his feet. Slow clicking of puzzle pieces in his mind said all of that was right. What he'd been wearing earlier, with his dark blue pork pie hat...

There it was. On the rumpled sheets of the bed next to him, where even now Dr. John was glaring and leaping down to go find someplace quieter to sleep.

Heath's dry mouth tasted like stale hazelnut coffee and chocolate donuts. That wasn't so good. How many of those things had he eaten?

And why was he awake?

The trilling beep came again.

Oh, yes. Heath's notebook computer, sitting open on the nightstand because Nariko was going to...

Nariko!

Sexy adrenaline pumped wakefulness through Heath's system as he spun to face the computer. He hoped his brown hair looked sleepy-sexy and not just messy. Smile already on his face, he swiped the right pattern across the screen to answer.

Nariko was someplace private. Orangish walls and yellowish light. Looked like one of those sliding paper doors behind her. Heath didn't know anyone still used those outside of theme restaurants.

More important was Nariko herself. Alone. Long black hair down and shimmering. She wore a red silk robe, tied at the waist by a sash in such a way that it covered her, yet left no doubt she was naked underneath.

This might just become the single best long distance call of Heath's life.

"Hi," Nariko said with a smile, her tone saying that the look on Heath's face was exactly the reaction she was shooting for. "Was that Dr. John's tail I saw disappearing into the hallway? Scritch him for me."

"Next time I see him." Heath held up three fingers as though he'd been a Boy Scout. "Promise."

"So..." Nariko drew out the word while her fingers played with the sash of her robe. "Have you been a good boy?"

Yes. The obvious answer was yes. Colin would tell him to say yes. Heath's own body begged him to say yes.

One simple word. Just a syllable, really. All he had to do was say that word and this conversation could take some wonderful turns. Important turns, really. Heath had two heaps of trouble waiting outside his front door, and how could anyone blame him for wanting to face those troubles relaxed and happy?

Surely the right thing to do here was say yes. Just let that word drip off the tip of his tongue. He could do it, too. Easiest thing in the world...

Except.

Except that he'd be lying.

Not to a priest. Not to an enemy. Not to a client.

He'd be lying to Nariko.

Three times Heath and Nariko had broken up and gotten back together. Four, maybe, though Heath really didn't want that number to be four.

Nariko was lying about why she was in Japan. Or at least, she wasn't telling Heath the whole truth about her trip. And wasn't saying yes here and now only doing the same thing? Holding back a little of the truth when there was nothing the other person could do to help anyway? Wasn't it just about keeping the other person from worrying needlessly?

That might have been true. If Heath weren't worried about Nariko. About whatever dangerous thing she was doing over there and not telling him about.

This wasn't going to work. Them. The two of them. Heath and Nariko. Nariko and Heath. They were never going to make it as a couple if they kept lying to each other. For convenience. To spare each other.

For their own immediate gains.

"No," Heath said with a sigh. "I'm sorry, Nari. I want so badly to say yes to that question. But I need to tell you about my morning because I love you too much to lie to you. There have been too many lies between us. Too many things held back. That needs to stop."

Heath looked up, expecting to see fury in her eyes. Expecting to see her cinch her robe tight. Maybe even see her mouth open as a prelude to the imprecations that would inevitably follow.

But her eyes were shiny. Almost misty. And her voice was soft when she said, "It's okay, baby. Tell me what's going on."

TELLING NARIKO THE TRUTH DIDN'T TAKE AS LONG AS HEATH'D expected.

He couldn't have been sitting on the edge of his bed, dumping out everything that had happened that morning — and catching her up on Drake's declaration of war — for more than ten minutes.

Meanwhile, she'd turned her tablet around so Heath could see that she was sitting on the edge of a bed too.

Two beds between them, and nothing sexy going on. The Lwa were definitely laughing at Heath now.

When Heath finished, his last words hung in the air for a moment. As though they'd needed time to travel the internet to Nariko before they settled in and she could understand them.

Finally, Nariko chuckled, soft and humorless.

"Let me guess," Heath said, "I'm—"

"Actually," Nariko said, "I was going to say I can't leave you alone for a moment, can I?"

"Hey." Heath sat a little straighter. "I didn't say I couldn't handle this. I've got everything under control here. Why? How is your secret project going?"

Nariko's face started to blank, but then she sighed and looked more tired than Heath had ever seen her.

"It's not. I thought I'd found a way out from under my mom's thumb, but" — Nariko sighed and shook her head — "it's not going to work."

"Are you ever going to tell me what the deal is between you and your mom?"

"Yes," she said, nodding so slowly it was like she had to lift the whole sky with her head. "But not today."

"Nariko—"

"No, Heath." She raised her hand in a halting gesture. "I don't doubt you can kick Drake's ass, and I expect you to get that taken care of. Pronto."

"Well, of course," Heath said, "I just—"

"Because," Nariko continued, "you need that wrapped up before we figure out how we're going to take down Vizinha."

"We?"

"Yep. I'm grabbing a flight home. Colin or — Tony was it? — can pick me up at the airport tomorrow morning and we'll all have a strategy session at Colin's at noon tomorrow." She arched an eyebrow. "I assume you can be rested and ready?"

"Believe it."

"That's what I like to hear."

"But why Colin's?"

"Simple," she said with a smile. "He buys better coffee than you do, and when I'm along he won't make that hazelnut crap. Besides..." Nariko played her fingers along the edges of her robe. "I don't want to see the inside of your place again until it's safe to jump your bones."

Her tone was light, but Heath wasn't ready to relax that much. Not yet.

"I know you're in the middle of something, Nari. I don't know what it is. I mean, I know it's more than visiting family. But—"

Nariko started laughing. It wasn't a happy laugh.

"Oh ... oh, Heath. All I'm doing is visiting family. It's just that, baby, when all this is over, I'm going to have to tell you a few things about my family."

7

Just before Heath left his apartment an hour later, he did the one thing he hated to do above almost all things in life — he put on a suit.

That he had a suit at all was a testimony to the strength of his grandmother's ability to nag cross-country. She'd insisted that a Cyr boy had to have a suit ready at all times, just in case he had to go to a wedding or a funeral, and "the latter don't give you no warning, boy."

He'd refused to spend more than he had to on an article of clothing he'd never wanted to own and certainly never intended to wear, no matter how scandalized his grandmother would be if she knew.

He'd just have to keep her from finding out.

So instead of going to a proper store for a proper fitted suit, he'd grabbed something off the rack at the nearest thrift store. It was a faded burgundy color and hung so loose Heath could probably have fit two of himself inside it. The white shirt he'd gotten at the same store hadn't been white in a very long time, and the tie had a paisley pattern of dark colors that probably hid a few food stains if anyone looked close enough.

All told, they looked bad on him, and they smelled worse. Like they'd spent a decade in mothballs before someone had thought to donate them. Might even have come from the estate of a dead man.

Heath had ways of finding out those things, if he'd wanted to know. And in this case, he really didn't want to know.

But Heath could honestly tell his grandmother that he owned a suit. And that woman could tell when he was lying. Well, when he was telling a direct lie, anyway. One good thing the path of conjure had done for Heath was give him a fluid relationship with the truth, as it pertained to most things in life.

Not something he wanted to think too much about right then, because it might just make him wonder how long this new honesty between himself and Nariko was going to last.

The important thing was that Heath had a suit that he didn't really think of as his. Someone else had owned and worn it for a good long time before it had come into his hands. Someone who might not even be numbered among the living these days.

Same was true for that shirt — honestly, who needed a long-sleeved shirt on the west coast? — and for that tie.

No one would ever associate any of the clothes on his body with Heath Cyr. Not even the worn leather dress shoes Heath had gotten on the same day at the same place.

He put on glasses with plain glass lenses, changed the part in his hair, and doubted anyone looking for Heath Cyr would look twice at him.

Especially since he'd left his backpack at home. He felt naked without it, but anyone who knew anything about Heath Cyr knew he carried a black canvas backpack. He left his phone and wallet at home too. Anything that could be identified with him. A small amount of cash in his pocket would take care of transportation.

Thus attired, Heath stepped outside and started sweating imme-diately in the midday heat. High 80s, had to be, and here Heath was stuck in all this fabric.

No. Not Heath. That was the point.

Soon as his front door was locked, Heath hustled his way out of the backyard and up the driveway to the public sidewalk. There he scattered a handful of poppy seeds and red pepper while spinning around thirteen times.

As he spun, he muttered, "Johnny Nobody" over and over.

Finally, he slipped a small paper packet out of the inside pocket in his jacket. A good, strong *ignore-me* charm. He licked the tip of his right pinky and rubbed the center of the packet to wake up the spirit of the charm, then slipped it back into his jacket pocket and started walking. Head down, and hands in his jacket pockets.

The streets in Heath's neighborhood were almost like a great big park, if he ignored the cars. Kids running and playing. Joggers and hikers and bicyclists out for their exercise. Lots of Oregon native plants growing in the yards — far more wild yards than grass yards in his neighborhood — and plenty of trees.

But then, the whole city often felt like a forest to Heath.

Sometimes he loved that. But today it made him miss the bustle of Manhattan. Heath's disguise would have been perfect in Manhattan. Just one more among the thousands of pedestrians lost in their own worlds as they quick-marched toward their destinations.

Here though, he didn't look like he was on his way to Forest Park for a hike, so without the *ignore-me* charm he might have drawn attention to his awful suit.

As it was, no one had even said a word to him by the time he boarded a MAX light rail train bound farther up into the hills, going west toward Beaverton. Because of course Drake lived in Beaverton.

Not that there was anything wrong with Beaverton, per se. It was just that ... it didn't feel like Portland. It felt more like ... it reminded Heath of the Bay Area expatriates who'd settled there. Heath had once spent a week down around San Francisco and San Jose, and he would have sworn that Beaverton was one of the suburbs from that area just plucked up and dropped down in Oregon.

And thinking about Beaverton helped Heath not think about the urine smell from someone's MAXident. He was grateful for the odor, in a way, because it made most of the patrons seek other cars when he didn't really want company. But that didn't mean *he* wanted to smell it either.

Apart from the odor, the train car was nice. Recent. Decent padding on the hard plastic seats, and the floors were hardly sticky at all. Would've felt like heaven back in Manhattan, especially with almost the whole train to himself. He never saw anything close to that on a subway car.

The train went up the hills, then through the tunnel where Heath had the distinct impression that something big and nasty had set up shop. Every time he took the MAX through the tunnel he got that same cold feeling in the pit of his stomach, like he was a fly zipping all too close to the spider's web.

But no spider caught him. And the train sped its way past the Rose Garden and the Portland Zoo and on into Beaverton, where Heath finally got off the train.

Fewer trees here. Made the city feel hotter and the streets smell dirtier. Though that might just have been Heath's mood. The streets seemed busier too. More fumes and exhaust from more cars, even though Heath came out of the station onto a relatively minor side street.

Finding Drake's place had been almost embarrassingly easy. The guy was part of a few meet-up websites, and offered apprenticeships in "LHP" out of his home.

Apparently that meant Left Hand Path.

Apparently *that* meant a kind of selfish approach to Western Ceremonial magic that, as far as Heath could tell from perusing a couple of internet forums, was mostly mental masturbation from the kind of "occultists" who loved to show up and argue theory at Croatoan — Maggie's other bar — without having enough magical *oomph* to pop a paper bag.

Drake had that kind of *oomph*. That was why he could find Gripper, much less get allowed in to drink. At least, when he wasn't making death threats. But maybe he liked to attend Croatoan too. No doubt for the same reason he placed ads for "apprentices."

All just excuses to meet young, nubile, and most importantly impressionable women. Or maybe men. Heath didn't know Drake's proclivities, and he didn't particularly care.

What mattered most was that he'd found Drake's home address.

And now Heath had found the house.

EVEN IF HEATH HADN'T KNOWN THE ADDRESS, HE WOULDN'T HAVE HAD any trouble spotting Drake's house on this block. Well, he might have, if he'd come hunting for it during the Halloween season. Of course, even then he would have spotted Tony's Forester parked at the curb out front.

The house sat at the end of the block, with an L of tall redwood privacy fences to keep the neighboring houses from watching whatever lascivious rites he conducted "skyclad" in his backyard. But facing the street was a tall, wrought iron fence, complete with spikes. Had a side-rolling gate at the driveway that looked automatic, and a gate over the front walk with a buzzer call box.

The fence also had three signs posted above the buzzer, all with burnt lettering into walnut wood. The topmost: "Within this place are the secrets of the universe laid bare." The middle: "Let all who come within bring no harm with them, lest that harm be visited on their heads a thousand fold." The bottom: "No solicitors."

The front lawn was well-cropped grass, and Heath couldn't help losing a moment imagining Drake's saggy butt in jeans and a stained white tee shirt, pushing an old-school, mechanical lawnmower.

He stopped the image before he laughed.

The house itself stood two stories tall. It was painted black, with red trim, which his neighbors must have *loved*. Lots of windows, all with what looked like blackout drapes shut tight. Big front porch, but no chairs or tables. Apparently Drake wasn't the kind of guy who liked to sit on his front porch in the evening and watch the world go by.

But whatever he did with his garage, he didn't use it to store his car. Black Ferrari Testarossa on the poured concrete driveway. So nice it gleamed. Heath didn't know cars all that well, but it looked either brand new or recently detailed.

License plate read MAGUS. Not *that* new then.

Heath could feel the wards on this place itching at his skin, even though he stood on the sidewalk outside them. So many and with so much power thrust into them the air almost buzzed. Wards against thieves. Wards against vandals. Wards against accidents. Wards against enemy spells.

If Heath were willing to open his spirit eyes, no doubt he'd see them as bubbles of force. But that would have taken time he didn't want to spend. He was walking slowly like he was looking for an address, staring hard at every house he passed, and he could only stare at this one so long before the behavior might start pushing the spirit of his *ignore-me* charm.

Charms like that one were terrific at what they did, as long as the person using them didn't do something stupid like ring Drake's buzzer and run.

That was only a flash of temptation. Honest.

Heath knew what else he'd see if he opened his spirit eyes: spirits. He could feel them moving through the air above him. Like a pulling in his gut, giving him a sense of where they were and how big and bad they were.

Compared to the ones Drake had sent to Heath's place, these little things were nothing. Just watchers, doing what watchers did: watch. They felt like guard dogs, and how he knew that wasn't something he could ever have put into words. It was like the spirits had a different taste to them, and these tasted more like watch dog types.

Not that Heath made a habit of licking spirits. Which was why he usually refused to answer when people asked how he could tell one type from another with his spirit eyes closed.

But Heath wasn't here to cause harm. He was here to slip a little something past Drake's defenses. A little something to make easier what Heath wanted to do later.

Heath pulled two eggs out of his jacket pocket. They were eggs he'd poked holes in, drained, and then filled with powder before sealing with a drop of glue each. Technique he'd used a thousand times.

The first egg he lobbed over the gate and toward the Ferrari. It smashed just shy of the driver's door, scattering red-brown powder where the driver had no choice but to step in it.

The second egg he threw just shy of the porch, where it smashed open and scattered its powder on the front walk.

Heath then put his head down, his hands in his pockets, and went back to walking as though he were looking for an address.

And as soon as he made it around the block he headed straight back for the MAX train.

HEATH WENT HOME AND SHOWERED AWAY THE MOTHBALL SMELL BEFORE even checking his phone messages.

Two from Colin. Three from Tony. That sounded about right. Heath sat on his bed in his red fuzzy bathrobe, scritching Dr. John's belly while listening to his messages.

First from Tony: "It's Brother Antonio, Heath. I thought you were going to give me time to talk some sense into Drake before doing anything you couldn't take back. This powder, Heath. What's in it? What have you done? I ... I stepped in it too. Whatever you're doing, Heath, you're doing it to me too. Is that really what you want? Call me."

First from Colin: "Hey, um, Heath? Not that I'm questioning your methods or anything, but I thought you said you were just joking about what you were going to do to Drake. You know. What you told Tony? Call me, all right?"

Second from Tony: "Brother Antonio again, Heath. Tony. You haven't called me back yet. Please, call me back. I'm not kidding. We both stepped in that powder. My brother called Vizinha, but he couldn't get a straight answer out of her. Look. I know you said you'll do what it takes to end this quickly, but ... you wouldn't really do that to me too? I cannot claim to be an innocent man in the eyes of the Lord, Heath, but I have done *nothing* to you. Please. Stop this before it's too late."

Second from Colin: "So ... you still haven't called me back. What's going on? Seriously. I'm getting monks calling me left and right looking for you. I've got Tony in one ear going on about how you're going to kill him too, and Brother Theodopolis in the other about how they haven't found any cures for the zombie magic and *do I know any*? That's not really what you're doing, is it, Heath? Please. Call me. For the love of Tigger, call me."

Third from Tony: "He'll apologize, Heath. Mandrake has sworn to me as a priest that he will meet you at seven o'clock this evening at Gripper to publicly rescind his threat and apologize to you. I even bore witness while he made arrangements with the bar's owner. I believe he's serious, and I think you should too. If you take this step, Heath, you may not be able to turn from that path. So please, please, for the love that Christ bears all sinners, please at least give my brother the chance to make good on his promise before it's too late. For all three of us."

Heath smiled and breathed a deep sigh of satisfaction.

"What do you think, Doc?" Heath said, scratching his cat's belly a little more vigorously and getting a stronger purr for his efforts. "Should I let them stew a little more first?"

Dr. John stretched, which Heath interpreted as a yes.

"You're evil," he said with a chuckle.

The cat regarded him through half-open eyes as though to say, "not to you."

Heath chuckled again.

He fired off a text message to Tony: "Got your messages. All right. Everything's on hold. For now."

His phone rang immediately. Tony calling. Heath didn't answer.

"Can't talk," he texted back. "Need to focus on this or something might go wrong."

He flopped back onto the bed next to his cat. Dr. John purred louder, rolled over, and started kneading Heath's side through the robe. Tiny pinpricks of his claws just getting through with each pass.

"You need a trim, big guy," Heath said, scritching the soft black fur behind his cat's ears.

Next a text message to Colin: "Don't tell anyone it's me. Call me if you're alone."

His phone rang immediately. Heath barely pushed the button to answer before Colin's worried voice met him.

"Heath. What the hell's going on, man? Vizinha called me. *Fucking Vizinha called me.*"

Heath sat up. "She did?"

Dr. John mewed irritation that Heath stopped paying attention to him. Heath absently reached down and resumed petting the cat as he and Colin spoke.

"Yes! She gave me a message for you. She thinks a dark Heath is a sexy Heath, and she wants to have dinner with you tonight."

Heath didn't even know how to respond to that. So instead he asked the less important question.

"Why does Vizinha have your phone number?"

"Please, a woman that hot asks for my phone number she gets it. Not like I've got a steady relationship these days." Then Heath would have sworn he could hear Colin shake himself on the other end of the line. "What the hell is going on?"

Heath chuckled. "I learned some bad habits from my uncle, and it's true he's just about as evil a man as you'll find anywhere on this globe. But I did learn a few useful things from him."

"Like how to make zombies?"

"Like that the best lies are the ones with some truth in them, and that the best feints are the ones that can become real attacks if the enemy ignores them."

"Is any of this going to become English anytime soon?"

"One condition," Heath said, holding up an index finger that Colin couldn't see. "If I answer this question, you can't talk to Tony until after that seven o'clock meeting."

"So you've spoken to Tony?"

"Not directly. And if I tell you what's going on, you can't talk to him either. Brother Theodopolis either. No more chatting with monks. Not until tonight."

"Fine. Now what's going on?"

Heath smiled and started to explain.

8

THE CEMETERY WAS DARK, AND SMELLED OF MOSS AND FRESH-DUG graves. Night sky full of stars overhead, but the moon was dark. New. The wind wasn't strong, but it bit, considering Heath was clad only in his red fuzzy bathrobe. Not much grass grew between the graves, but what there was grew dry, strewn with weeds and crabgrass and stones under Heath's bare feet. One leafless, gnarled oak tree anchored the center of the graveyard, a rotted noose still hanging from a broad branch.

Heath was looking for something. He knew that much. And whatever it was lay here among the weathered marble and crumbling stone of these old graves that still looked and smelled so fresh.

That didn't make sense. How could these graves be old, but look and smell fresh? And why was it nighttime? And why was Heath only in his red...

Dreaming. Had to be.

That realization snapped him into lucidity. Gave him fresh eyes to look at the graveyard around him. A cemetery, yes, but not one he knew. Not one he'd ever been to, nor seen pictures of. Cemeteries sometimes appeared in Heath's dreams, but they always looked like the big, fancy ones around New Orleans. Full of swampy, bayou smells and fancy stone mausoleums that locked with wrought iron gates.

This graveyard looked spookier. Gave Heath a fluttery feeling down in his gut, plus that itch at the back of his neck that suggested he was being watched.

This wasn't part of his personal dreamscape then. Something from the broader area of the dream worlds.

Did it belong to one of the Ghedes? Was Brav finally looking for his flask?

No. This didn't look like the place between, where Heath met Ghede Brav last month. This place had the feel of a crossroads to it. A true crossroads. A choice point you can't change your mind about a mile or two down, not without backtracking all the way back to select a different route.

No, there was something about the graves. The fresh dirt in old graves. Something ... compelling about them.

Heath knelt down over one. The marker was old gray stone, crumbling around the edges, with the name worn away by years and rains. There was something in the ground here, though. Something under that freshly turned earth.

Power.

Power in the ground here. Not special place power, like some of the spots around Portland. No, this wasn't power of the land. This was power of the grave. Power of *this* grave. And each of the other graves all around Heath, and there were dozens of them in this small ceme-tery, each of them had their own power too.

Dozens of graves here. Two or three score of them, all told. Each of them with their own secrets and their own power. And all of it could be Heath's for the taking...

That sense of being watched grew stronger. Heath could feel a presence behind him.

He turned without rising.

A gaunt man in rumpled finery. Skin so dark Heath's father and uncle would look pale by comparison. Top hat and tails to go with the suit pants, but a cheap shirt under the black tuxedo vest, and scuffed dress shoes. White gloves and a diamond-studded cane all the same, though the diamond gleamed purple, not white. Sunglasses missing a lens, and the eye that showed had an iris as black as its pupil.

The man stood with feet apart, cane centered in front of him with both gloved hands on the purple diamond stud.

"Feel it, don't you, twilight boy?" The man had a voice like branches creaking in the wind, but there was something charismatic in his tone. "You can feel what's waiting in those graves. Waiting to help you out."

The man smiled, and that smile showed all the teeth of a bare skull.

"Yes, you feel that power. I know you do. You always did. Made your uncle jealous, not that he'd ever say so." The man tilted his head slightly to one side. "You know who I am, don't you, twilight boy?"

"Yes, I know who you are." Just thinking the name sent jitters all through Heath's nerves, but he had to say it aloud. "You're Baron Samedi."

"Very good." Baron Samedi gave a half-bow. "Now don't you be giving me that scaredy-cat look, twilight boy. Taught you a few things over the years, now haven't I? And you've been proper in your thanks, offering me molasses and rum every now and again."

Heath nodded slowly. While he'd never been in a position to have a conversation with the Baron before, he had picked up a few tricks over the years that had been inspired by the Baron.

Just exactly the kind of thing Heath had tried to explain to Tony. *Gris-gris.* Gray-gray. The Baron wasn't evil and he wasn't good, but he had a powerful dark side to him.

Just as concerning right now was the fact that the Baron was calling him "twilight boy." Some people called Heath "Twilight," but only Maggie's grandmother called him "twilight boy." She meant it as a kind of backhanded racist slap, Heath was pretty sure. So why would the Baron call him that?

"You're in a fix right now, aintcha, twilight boy?" The Baron began twirling his cane slow and easy, passing it back and forth between his hands without the spin so much as pausing. "Seems to me this is no time to be shy and scaredy. This is the time to take a little more control of your own destiny than you've been allowing yourself to take. Wouldn't you say so?"

"I'd say I'm doing all right," Heath said, though he kept his tone guarded. "I've got this Drake problem under control, and—"

Baron Samedi spat, and where his spittle hit the dirt a corpse flower bloomed a yard tall.

"I ain't talking about some no-account white boy demon fucker. You know just who I'm talking about."

"Vizinha," Heath said.

"That's the girl. Speaking of," — the Baron pointed his cane at Heath — "you should fuck her."

"*What?*" Heath shook his head in disbelief.

"A girl like that wants 'dinner' she's telling you just exactly what kind of sausage she wants passing between her lips." The Baron started slowly thrusting his hips. "And I mean both sets of lips."

"No!" Heath shook his head even harder. "Even if I weren't with Nariko. Just. No."

"See, that's just what I'm talking about."

Baron Samedi stopped thrusting his hips. Jabbed the dirt with his cane. And the corpse flower turned and looked at Heath, as though it had eyes to see with, and it was judging him.

"You're too uptight, twilight boy," the Baron said with another skull-like grin. "You throw that girl a bone and do it right, and she might let her guard down. Great chance to get her pretty boy *djab* away from her. Just tell your girlfriend you're taking one for the team."

"You don't seriously think I'd do that." Heath blinked. "Wait. No. You don't, do you. You know I wouldn't do it. And you know it wouldn't work. Vizinha's too careful."

Heath sighed so hard his shoulders and neck sagged.

"You're fucking with me. Aren't you?"

Baron Samedi brayed out loud laughter, and the corpse flower began to cackle.

"'Course I'm fucking with you. You're too serious, twilight boy. Never trust a serious man with power. He's sure to abuse it."

"And you *don't* want that?"

"Hell no." The Baron tipped his top hat back with the diamond of his cane. "'Course what you think of as abuse might not be what *I* think of as abuse. But it's not your fault you're wrong. You're still young."

"Old enough to know better than to let anyone tell me right from wrong," Heath said as he stood. "Even a Lwa."

More brays and cackles of laughter.

"That's *right*." Baron Samedi thumped his cane like applause. "That's just exactly right, twilight boy. You don't need me telling you right from wrong, any more than you need Legba or Damballah doing it. You're a grown-ass man who can make his own grown-ass decisions. And that's just exactly why I called you here."

Heath looked at all the graves surrounding him. All those graves brimming with power.

"You want to teach me to make zombies?"

More laughter yet. In the middle of it, the Baron spat again. Now he was flanked by cackling corpse flowers in his humor.

"Zombies are only one of the things I can teach you. And just between us and these here graves, the best stuff doesn't get talked about anywhere. You work with me and a year from now you'll think of zombies as kid stuff."

Heath shuddered.

"Please understand, Baron. I hold you in the highest regard. But I'm not sure I'm the man to learn what you have to teach. Heck, I'm not even sure I've been through the right initiations to handle it. But even if I had, I think my answer would still have to be no."

The Baron tilted his head, and used his cane to tip his hat a counterpoint direction.

"You sure about that, twilight boy? Might not survive what's coming for you. Not without my help."

Heath drew a deep breath and gave a single, firm nod. "I'm sure."

"You might want to think a little harder about that. I've seen what's coming your way."

"You heard him, Samedi," said a voice from off to Heath's left. A voice high and soft, whispery and thin. A voice Heath hadn't heard for quite some time. "Boy says no then the boy means no."

Heath turned to see an old man approaching. Bent over a bit with the weight of years and using a cane, but stepping lively all the same. His skin was almost as dark as the Baron's, and he wore the simple, frayed clothes of a farmhand. Or maybe a slave. His eyes were the brown of whip leather, but they held a bit of sparkle.

Papa Legba.

"Nobody called you here, Legba," the Baron said, waving his cane in dismissal. "Go find someone else to bother."

"This boy and I have an old agreement." Papa Legba stopped maybe three steps from the Baron. "And while I don't mind sharing, I do mind poaching. He says no, I say you have to respect that."

"I am respecting it." Baron Samedi pointed at Heath with his cane. "I'm just saying that the boy ought to consider changing his mind, and that if he does all he needs to do is let me know."

"So you said that then." Papa Legba thumped his cane four times, slow and steady.

The Baron started to say something, but Papa Legba cut in ahead of him.

"You said your piece." He thumped his cane again, the same way. Four beats. Slow and steady. "And the boy's said his."

Four more thumps.

"And I say," — Papa Legba stepped forward again — "that this conversation is *over*."

He thumped his cane four more times.

9

HEATH AWOKE TO THE SOUND OF SOMEONE KNOCKING. HIS HEAD ACHED, his stomach growled, and his eyes were full of sleep. His mouth was dry and he could still taste hints of that hazelnut from Colin's coffee. He knew he'd dreamed something, but for the life of him he couldn't remember what.

He was still naked except for his red bathrobe. Dr. John curled up and happily sleeping away on his chest.

"This is your doing, isn't it?" Heath said to his cat. "I didn't get enough sleep last night, so you lulled me into napping."

The cat ignored him and kept sleeping.

The knock came again. Four beats to it, even measure and even pressure. Something about it echoed in Heath's mind, but he didn't know why. It was a very orderly knock, and very unlike anyone Heath knew who could make it to his front door these days without him knowing in advance.

A recent surprise midnight visit from Heath's landlord had made him take a few extra security precautions, but whoever was on Heath's front porch hadn't set off any of them. So they didn't present any kind of threat, expressed or implied.

Dr. John stretched, rolled over, blinked at Heath, and went back to sleep.

"You're no help," Heath said. Then raised an eyebrow. "Or are you? I mean, that's not Colin. Nariko won't be back from Japan for —Heath glanced at the analog clock on his nightstand which told him it was just after four — more than sixteen hours. And the last thing I need at the moment is another client."

Heath stretched and eased back down into the soft cotton sheets.

"Whoever it is can go away."

The knock came again. This time it was followed by a sedate voice that somehow managed to carry through the door and down to the hall, yet sound almost as though the speaker were right next to Heath.

"My patience has been tested by our Lord many times, Mr. Cyr. Do not expect to best it with indolence."

Heath sighed. He recognized that voice. Brother Theodopolis.

"Sorry," Heath said to Dr. John as he dislodged the now-disgruntled cat. Heath pulled his robe tighter and scuffed his bare feet down the hardwood floor to the front door.

He opened the front door and there stood Brother Theodopolis. A thin man, but broad through the jaw and shoulders. He had a crooked nose that had clearly been broken more than once, and a square-ish head that made the choice of a tonsure look ... unfortunate. But there was no point in telling the monk to grow out the rest of his white hair. He wouldn't have listened to fashion advice, his wardrobe was proof of that. He was dressed in what Heath was starting to think of as "monk chic" — all black, and more wool than anyone should wear in this heat, especially with the humidity on the rise.

"Brother Theodpolis," Heath said by way of greeting before stepping past the monk onto the front porch, and closing the door behind him.

Brother Theodopolis looked at the door then back at Heath.

"Policy," Heath said. "I don't discuss business in the house." He sat in one of the plastic chairs on his porch and pointed to the other. "And I don't think you're here for personal reasons."

"That is an interesting conundrum," Brother Theodopolis said, not yet taking a seat. "Souls are my business, but nothing is more personal than the matters pertaining to one's soul."

"You're here about Drake?" Heath kept his tone gruff.

Brother Theodopolis tilted his head back and forth. "Yes and no. I am concerned about steps you've taken today, yes, but I am also here about how those matters affect your soul, as well as how they affect Brother Antonio, who is innocent in this matter."

"Sounds like business to me."

Brother Theodopolis turned his chair so it faced Heath dead on, and perched on the edge of it.

"The Heath Cyr I met a few short weeks ago would not have been willing to take so drastic a step as imprisoning the soul of another. In point of fact, I do not believe that man would have seriously entertained the notion of doing so. And yet I have had a friend of mine who is learned in the ways of alchemy go over the powder you used today. He assures me that it contains ingredients known to be used by *bokors* in their zombie poisons."

Heath gave the monk an absolute stone wall of a straight face.

"It disturbs me, Mr. Cyr, that you even know the ingredients to such a poison."

"I know a lot of things I'd be happier not knowing." Heath shrugged. "The key to conjure isn't what you know, it's knowing when and how to *use* what you know. Do I want Drake's ugly soul flitting around my house for the next twenty years? Not especially. But he pushed my hand, and I just don't have time to play things subtle. Too many people are counting on the next item on my agenda."

"And that justifies doing the same thing to Brother Antonio? A man who has only worked to diffuse the matter? A man who would place himself in harm's way to aid you?"

"Well..." Heath said, turning slightly to the side so he could stretch his legs and cross them at the ankle without accidentally giving the monk a show. "I haven't done anything yet that I can't provide an antidote for. And besides, my aim's got a pretty good track record. I reckon I could take down Drake right now and not even make Tony puke up his lunch."

"Mr. Cyr." Brother Theodopolis sighed. "My brothers and I want to believe you are a good man. We want to believe you are an ally to us in our crusade against the dark powers of this earth. But what you are saying does not reassure me. In fact, I find it persuasive that you are coming to ally yourself with those dark powers instead."

That made Heath sit up straight. He could almost hear his grandmother screaming at him clear from the other side of the country.

He looked Brother Theodopolis in the eye and saw only patience and sadness...

But there was something off. Just a hair. Something in the monk's posture. If he believed what he was saying, he should have been more rigid through the shoulders. A little tighter through the neck.

Maybe the monk was just that confident. Or maybe...

Heath narrowed his eyes.

"When did you figure it out?"

"Just now," Brother Theodopolis said, breathing out a long sigh and easing back in his chair. "I didn't want to believe it, but you've been very persuasive."

"It's the nature of my work," Heath said, dismissively, then leaned forward, a little more intense. "So you weren't sure. Why come alone? Why risk confronting me?"

"Faith," Brother Theodopolis said as though it were the most obvious thing in the world.

"So now what? You gonna tell Tony?"

"No," Brother Theodopolis said with a firm shake of his head. "I assume you have your reasons for keeping your secrets. But I will need to tell my order the truth, if we are to continue to work with you from time to time."

"Fine." Heath stood. "You better come inside then. Hard to get more personal than this stuff."

ONCE THEY WERE SEATED AT HEATH'S KITCHEN TABLE AND EACH MAN had a cold bottle of Teufelsbrau Dark in his hand, Heath began to tell Brother Theodopolis what was going on.

"But before I go any further, let's get something clear. I don't answer to you or yours. I answer to higher authorities than you, and while I like having you guys as casual allies, don't think I'm going to start explaining myself every time I take a step you don't agree with."

"Why tell me anything then?" Impressive patience in that monk's voice.

While he decided how to answer, Heath took a swig of his beer. Dark and rich with just a little bite.

"I like you. And I like Tony." He sighed. "And yeah, some of it is because I'll need your help with Vizinha. Assuming you're still willing to help."

"That remains to be seen."

Heath raised an eyebrow.

"As you say, Mr. Cyr." Brother Theodopolis took a long pull from his beer. "You are not beholden unto us, nor are we answerable to you." Brother Theodopolis gave Heath a small, sly smile. "Besides, isn't that a business matter?"

"Fair enough. I'll tell you this much for free, though, because if everything blows up in my face, I want the record clean. I don't call zombies. I haven't even asked the Baron for permission, much less specific instructions in how it's done."

"But the powder—"

"Contains a lot of the same elements I'd use for about six different hexes." Heath waggled his eyebrows. "Conjure isn't alchemy. Our recipes ... get a little fluid."

"So it *was* part of an attack."

"Not yet." Heath sipped his beer. "I did it for the bluff. Because Tony was there. Because I knew someone would figure out what was in the powder. And because with my uncle's visit to town so fresh in everybody's minds, there'd be no doubt I could get it done if I decided to."

"So, under the guise of truce, you used Brother Antonio as a tool of misinformation against his own brother."

"I did specify he wasn't representing me in any way, so there wasn't any truce crap. As for the rest" — Heath shrugged — "he put himself in the middle of this. That's the risk he took."

Brother Theodopolis started to say something, but Heath spoke over him.

"Besides. He desperately wanted a nonviolent solution. I gave him one. *If* Drake follows through on the apology and such."

"But Drake will learn nothing from this except to choose his opponents more carefully in the future."

"Not my concern."

Brother Theodopolis considered that while both men worked on their beers.

"What if the ruse hadn't worked?"

"I told you that already." Heath smiled. "I know at least six different hexes I could work from the powder Drake already touched."

"And if they affected Brother Antonio?"

"Nah." Heath finished his beer. "I've got better aim than that. And I'm *hoping* it won't come to that."

"But you aren't sure."

"Nothing's sure until Drake says his piece at Gripper tonight."

"Has it occurred to you that he might be luring you into a trap?"

"Of course," Heath said as though *that* were the most obvious thing in the world. "Not at the bar itself, of course, but between here and there."

"Why not there? A comfortable, social environment. You'll be off your guard."

"At Gripper?" Heath said with a laugh. "No. I won't be off my guard. But he'd be risking the wrath of the other patrons, plus Maggie herself, who's no slouch. Not to mention that on Friday nights, Mrs. Halloran acts as bouncer."

"Mrs. Halloran?"

"Maggie's old-country Irish Witch of a grandmother. And you haven't seen scary until you've met that woman."

"But between here and there you'll be vulnerable."

"Oh, I don't know that I'd say *that*, exactly." Heath quirked a half-smile. "I do have my ways. And if he's stupid enough to try something, well ... let's just say that when I come back at him, the pump's already primed."

Brother Theodopolis finished his own beer then, and shook his head as he stood.

"I would not want you for an enemy, Mr. Cyr."

"Oh, I guess I can be a little tricky." Heath smiled as he stood. "For what it's worth, I wouldn't want you for an enemy either, Brother Theodopolis."

"You misunderstand me," Brother Theodopolis said as the two shook hands. The monk had a firm yet unchallenging handshake. "The darkness is too close to you. I fear you will not hesitate to step down that path, should you face a challenging enough situation. If we quarreled, I fear not what you would do to us, but what you would do to yourself. What you would become."

With that happy thought, Brother Theodopolis took his leave.

10

HEATH WOULD NEVER HAVE ADMITTED TO ANYONE — EXCEPT *MAYBE* Nariko, if this new honesty policy held between them — but Brother Theodopolis' words had gotten to him. Was he getting a little too quick to look to the darker side of *gris-gris*?

When all this was over, he needed to go see his family. Not his uncle. His mom and dad, and maybe his grandmother.

For the time being, though, he needed to put that out of his head. So, after he downed two microwaved pepperoni pizza calzones to appease his stomach, he spent an hour or more grinding and chopping raw herbs, drying others, and generally doing the kind of manual labor part of conjure that he found peaceful. Contemplative.

And if those herbs happened to be the ones he was likely to need against Vizinha, so much the better. Agrimony and Cruel Man of the Woods. High John the Conqueror, Devil's Shoestring, and lemon grass. Flax and garlic and black pepper and more.

Kept himself busy until it was just about time to go. Then he got dressed. Short-sleeved red-and-white striped shirt with buttons. Khaki cargo shorts and his brown leather boat shoes.

Then, Heath sighed and did something he avoided whenever possible — he picked up his car keys.

Heath hadn't driven at all as a teen, growing up in Manhattan where the subway was king. He'd learned because his parents insisted, and once he'd moved west he understood why. Most cities weren't built for public transit the way Manhattan was.

Portland came pretty close though, so Heath liked to encourage the system's growth by taking public transportation as often as possible.

Plus, Heath didn't care much for being stopped by the police, and cutting out driving was a key way to cut down on police interactions. And not having to deal with bicyclists while behind the wheel was a perk he savored.

But today, taking his car was the right thing to do.

Heath's car was a junked out old AMC Gremlin hatchback. The car had started life red, but over the years that red had faded to a color that Nariko called amaranth. Of course, she also called Heath's car "a heap" that "no self-respecting dump would take" and refused to even consider riding in it.

Clearly she failed to appreciate the purpose behind this hunk of junk.

Even without so much as a pinch of magic, this car was not one people wanted to notice. In fact, they tended to go out of their way to *not* notice it. Other drivers gave it a wide berth because it was ancient and dinged and could only have been driven by a driver unafraid to hit anything. Most observers would doubt it could *achieve* the speed limit, much less exceed it.

Heath called it the *Parakeet*, and liked to think of the car as his own personal *Millennium Falcon*. Looked like crap, but quietly upgraded in ways no one would ever guess.

Thanks to his own workings, cops were all but incapable of noticing the car, much less the man at the wheel. Other drivers forgot the car as soon as it passed. Oh, nothing that made the car invisible or anything. Nothing that would lead to accidents. In fact, accidents were one the things the car was charmed against.

It was just that the space this car occupied was deemed unworthy of attention by other drivers.

Same held true for pedestrians, thieves, meter maids and the like. Heath could practically park the car in the middle of the street and get away with it, if he wanted. Not to mention that the *Parakeet* now treated specially prepared tap water as high quality gasoline, and could hold itself together through anything this side of a volcanic eruption.

The *Parakeet* was Heath's own personal tank.

That was part of the reason he didn't like to drive it too much. He didn't want to get too used to feeling that safe when he was out and about. Could lead to a fatal mistake.

Right now, though, for this drive, Heath needed to feel safe. And he doubted there was a ghostie, demon, *djab* or much of anything that could find him when he was driving this car. And anything that managed to find him would have one hell of a time battering through its defenses.

The engine coughed to life after only five cranks of the key and a "pretty please with sugar on it." The car was fully capable of starting without effort, but the *Parakeet* knew just how valuable it was, and it had developed a bit of an attitude.

"I know, I know," Heath said, patting the cracked vinyl of the dashboard. "I don't drive you enough. But, baby, you know it's just because you're too nice to waste running out for a quart of milk."

The engine settled into a smoother rumble then, though it did still have a bit of a whine.

"Fine," Heath said. "When all this is done I'll take you on a good long drive. Down to California and back. We'll go look at the big sequoias and I'll pick up a few things I haven't gotten around to planting up here. Deal?"

The whine eased away. The engine almost purred now.

"That's my girl."

Heath eased the car down the driveway, out onto the street, and into downtown traffic. Late Friday afternoons were always busy in downtown Portland, especially in the summertime, but Heath barely had to spare the traffic a thought. Cars moved out of his way left and right. Even the bicyclists yielded to a car that might run them over.

Heath was across the river almost before he knew it, turning left off of Burnside onto a side street that looked about as likely to draw attention as Heath's car. Just one more minor side street off a major thoroughfare.

Heath pulled over and parked in front of the dog shit brown stucco building sandwiched between a salvage shop and a musical instruments store. A building with no windows, but a red door painted with what looked to passersby like a stylized number 4, in purple paint.

It was actually the symbol of Jupiter, from some musty grimoire or other, and it marked the bar known as Gripper. No other signs at all. No advertising. Nothing that would draw curious onlookers out for a drink.

The only clients the Gripper wanted were the ones who didn't need a sign to know the building for what it was — a gathering place for those who walked one of the paths of what people called magic.

Heath checked the clock on his phone. Six-fifty-four. He slipped the phone back into a pocket in his cargo shorts, then patted all his pockets to make sure he still had the conjure hands he might need, along with various herbs, powders and oils.

Just in case.

He glanced around the street. Several other cars parked on and near the block, but he wasn't sure if there were more than normal. He did see Colin's Saturn, which meant Colin was already inside scoping the scene for him.

Heath checked his phone. No messages, voice or text. No surprises so far then.

Then Heath drew three deep breaths, offered a quick prayer to Papa Legba, picked up his backpack, and got out of the car.

"HEATH! THANK GOD!"

From under the awning in front of the musical instrument store, Tony came running.

"Hi, Tony," Heath said with a smile, adjusting the backpack on his shoulder. "Don't worry. You're not in any danger from me."

"Never mind that now." Tony was sweating from more than the heat. His brow was furrowed and he kept glancing at the front door of Gripper and back at Heath. "The old woman at the door won't let me in."

Heath sighed. "Why not?"

"She says they don't admit monks or priests 'of the Catholic variety.'" Tony's hands kept folding and unfolding as he spoke. "I need to be in there, though. I got through to him today, Heath. Your threat cemented it, but even so. He's ready to change. I know it. But he needs me with him in this moment of crisis. Both as a man of faith and as his brother."

"I'll see what I can do," Heath said with a grimace, "but I have enough enemies as it is. I don't want to give Mrs. Halloran any excuses to come after me."

Tony nodded, distracted, but followed a step behind Heath as he approached the door. It was a Friday evening, so he knocked four times, and wondered why that number echoed in his head.

Mrs. Halloran opened the door, blocking the entrance.

She looked like the human equivalent of what people saw when they looked at Heath's car. Frail and old, seventy-five if she was a day under a thousand. Wrinkles all but translucent, her skin was so pale, and her silver gray locks dangled just down as far as her shoulders. Powdery-sweet perfume hung about her like a personal fog.

But she wore her emerald green dress like royal vestments. And if the dress didn't give away the truth of her, Mrs. Halloran's green eyes did. They were sharp enough to engrave diamonds. And the silver torc around her neck, twisted Celtic knot work, was the resting place of a familiar spirit with a nasty reputation.

"Well, well, the twilight boy returns to us so soon," she said with an Irish lilt. "Looks to some as though you've put the fear of God into that pasty doughboy, haven't you now?"

"Not to you though."

"You're a clever one, there's none who'd deny it. But a powerful one? Well, that's a thing I find myself a *little* less convinced of."

"Am I allowed in?"

She held up one hand, one eyebrow raised expectantly. Heath handed her his backpack.

"*Now* you're allowed in."

"And what about my friend Tony?" Heath pointed at the monk with his thumb. "He has a part to play in tonight's little drama."

"Ah, but drama does follow you, doesn't it, boyo? Well, my granddaughter has given leave for some of your drama to pass her threshold tonight, but the rest of it needs to wait without. And so does your monk."

"This is a place for practitioners. I've witnessed him banish a demon. A president of Hell."

"Oh, and Hell has presidents, does it now? Well, I can't say as that surprises me overmuch." She cocked her head a little to the side, a sly grin in her aspect not quite reaching her lips. "You're having the year for demons now, aren't you, twilight boy? Could be someone's trying to tell you something."

"This man," Heath said pointing more directly at Tony, "is my friend and an occultist in his own right. He deserves a place here."

"Your *friend* is a papist and allied with the same people who tried to drive the Pagans out of Ireland. To say nothing of their crusades and inquisitions. He can go back to Rome where his kind belongs."

"He's Drake's brother," Heath said, lowering his voice, "and Drake needs him for support tonight."

"If the pasty doughboy is worried that you'll start something he can't finish, he should know good and well by now not to worry about such things. Not here. Nothing gets started here at Gripper that I don't finish me own self."

She raised an eyebrow. "And I doubt you've gotten so full of yourself that you'd be willing to try me, but if you have..."

She gave Heath a small, cold smile.

Before Heath could say anything, Tony put a hand on his shoulder.

"Thank you for trying. It's clear that this woman is more inter-ested in fights and grudges than in doing her job."

"I don't believe I could have heard that right." For the first time, Mrs. Halloran looked past Heath and locked eyes with Tony. "Are you foolish enough to say I don't know my job?"

"I worked as bouncer in Los Angeles for two years," Tony said, challenge in his voice. "First rule of door duty is that it's about the club, not you. When you let people in, when you say no, you always do it because it's what's best for the club. There's no room for personal grudges, biases, and the like."

"There's many among our clientele who'd be all too happy to see a priest or monk meet an untimely end. Letting *you* in would be inviting conflict the bar doesn't need."

"In this town the Paleros and Santeros have a feud that goes back decades," Heath said. "But Maggie lets them all in here so long as they behave themselves. And they do."

"Let the monk in, *Mórai*," Maggie called across the room, using the nickname Heath had heard her call her grandmother many times. "If he's got enough juice to send a demon packing, he's welcome to drink here until he proves more trouble than he's worth."

"By that metric," Mrs. Halloran started, but Maggie cut in.

"Let Heath in too."

Mrs. Halloran stood aside.

* * *

WORD OF TONIGHT'S BIG EVENT MUST HAVE SPREAD PRETTY FAST through the greater Portland occult community. Usually the crowds didn't start showing up at Gripper until about nine, but here it was, not quite seven o'clock, and already the place was two-thirds full.

Lots of faces Heath knew. Some he could even call friends. Hár, the big Viking-looking guy with the honey blond hair and beard who could read his runes at least as well as Heath could read cards or cowries. He'd lost an eye in Afghanistan, but it hadn't slowed him down at all. As usual, Hár was drinking with Jamon.

Jamon had what he liked to call "the Sephardic look," which as far as Heath could tell meant he was a Jewish guy who looked vaguely Hispanic: straight black hair and a skin tone on the dark side of olive. Jamon practiced some kind of ancient Hebraic shamanism. Or at least, that was as much sense as Heath could make of Jamon's descriptions. Jamon got technical when he talked theory.

Hár and Jamon raised their beers in toast to Heath, and Heath gave them a smile and a nod. Jamon wouldn't be staying long, and neither would the handful of other Jewish practitioners here today. It was Friday, so they'd all leave before sunset.

Not that every face in the crowd was friendly. No doubt several in attendance wanted to see this blow up in Heath's face.

Heath especially noted he'd have to keep an eye on a corner table where DeAndre McDaniels and José Rodrigo-Montoya were drinking together. That wasn't good. Those two didn't like each other much more than they liked Heath. All three of them plied similar trades on the west side of the Willamette, and both of those two had lost customers to Heath.

DeAndre was an ex-gangbanger, the kind of big, fat man whose fat got solid with muscle. He was wearing a purple suit and, with his dark chocolate skin, could pull it off. The bald head and three gold rings completed his look. José looked every inch a Spanish gentleman in his dark gray suit. Not a hair out of place and not a wisp of stubble on his narrow cheeks.

DeAndre was a conjure worker too, and José was a Palero. Both of them were about a decade older than Heath, and they'd hated him since the day he moved to Portland. Even now they gave him cool glares.

Heath gave them a cool glare of his own before looking over the rest of the room.

Some cities may have been bigger melting pots in terms of ethnicities than Portland, but Heath doubted any of them had more varieties of magic.

From Taoist alchemy to Qabala/Kabballah/Cabala — Heath had met serious practitioners who insisted on one spelling or another and he wasn't going to quibble with any of them over their own arts. From the Paleros who practiced Palo Mayombe to the Nordic folk with their runes and their *Seidh*. From obscure Romanian folk magic to current Romany practices. Greek Pagans who worshiped Zeus or Aphrodite, and didn't get along with the Italian Pagans who worshiped Jupiter or Venus. From *Curanderos* to sorcerers to those who insisted on calling what they did "white magic" or "black magic" or "high magic" or "low magic." Some who spelled magic with a "k" on the end, and some who would bristle at having their Art called magic in the first place.

More practices than Heath had ever known existed before he started hanging out at the Gripper. But then, having seen Colin pull real magic out of weird '70s self-help books, nothing really surprised Heath anymore.

Seven large tables in the center of the bar area, painted the colors Cornelius Agrippa attributed to the planets in his books. Black, blue, red, yellow, green, orange and silver. Like they belonged as marshmallows in a breakfast cereal.

Heath could never get a straight answer out of Maggie why there were seven planets in this system instead of nine. Or eight, depending on how Agrippa might have felt about Pluto.

But there were seven. And tonight every one of those tables was full.

Some of the smaller, brown, square tables around the perimeter of the room still had empty seats enough to accommodate any latecomers.

The ceiling was painted as a star field: black, with swirls of red and blue for nebulae and scores of little lights for the stars. There were floodlights arrayed around the perimeter, if needed, but the little lights kept the bar feeling cozy without getting dim.

From the hidden speakers came the gentle strains of Celtic harp music. Maggie only played that when she was expecting trouble. Something about the harp she considered soothing. No conversation competing with the harp music right now. All eyes in the room were on Heath.

Heath smiled like he was arriving for the Oscars, looking just about as relaxed and confident as it was possible for him to look. And he figured he had a pretty good reason for that. So far, everything was going according to plan.

He did resist the urge to wave like some visiting monarch, or even straighten his shirt.

Instead Heath inhaled deeply of the smell of garlic fries, a Gripper specialty, and started for the bar with Tony in his wake. Quiet as the room was — just the music and now a little whispering — Heath could hear the floorboards creak under their shoes.

The bar itself had hundreds of star charts lacquered into place along the top and sides. Worn and scuffed, like they'd seen heavy action in their day. But the star charts were all intact, and safe under thick coats of lacquer.

Only three people seated at that bar. Colin, Drake and Vizinha.

Colin sat apart from the other two, and Heath would have known immediately that Colin was nervous even if both his legs hadn't been twitching like a 5th Street junkie. It was the clothing that tipped it. Torn up jeans instead of shorts, and Nike high-tops tied tight, in case he had to run. And his faded black shirt — sleeves and collar ripped off — bore the logo of Blue Öyster Cult. He only wore BÖC when he was nervous.

He had a glass of beer on the bar in front of him, untouched, and his eyes kept flitting to Vizinha. Though, admittedly, that might just have been because she looked good.

Vizinha wore a red chiffon dress that barely covered her slender curves and showed off her legs. She had more than enough smooth Brazilian beauty to work as a model, if she'd only been a few inches taller. She certainly had the poise and confidence for the work, and right now she was giving Heath the kind of smile he'd never seen from her before: inviting.

That smile made Heath feel like he was picking his steps through a live minefield.

Drake was wearing cargo pants a size too small and a black tee shirt with a swirly silver logo that looked like one of those demon sigils he was so fond of. Looked as though he'd washed what mousy brown hair he had left, and from the nicks on his jowls he'd probably shaved too. He didn't like the look Vizinha was giving Heath...

...oh, crap. Was this idiot jealous?

No. It couldn't have been that. Drake couldn't have actually been stupid enough to come after Heath just to get Vizinha's attention. That would just be too pathetic for words. No, Heath decided he was going to continue believing Drake's motivations were exactly what he'd claimed — that Heath had "gotten in his way" too many times, and "needed to pay the price."

Or however the hell he'd put it.

A tall glass of Deschutes Hefeweizen was waiting on the bar for Heath, right in front of Maggie. Maggie had a smile that made Heath feel a lot more comfortable. Of course, Maggie's smile had that effect on everyone, so far as Heath could tell.

Maggie had the kind of smile that could ease a roomful of tension, if she used it that way. Right now, that little smile was just aimed at Heath.

Sweet smile for someone who looked like an ex-boxer. Heath had never asked if Maggie actually was an ex-boxer, but she had the broken nose and the muscled kind of fitness under her black tee shirt and blue jeans that suggested she could give — and take — a pounding. She kept her red hair buzzed short, completing the image.

Maggie did make one concession to the traditional American ideas of femininity — a touch of eye makeup, to bring out her clear blue eyes.

"So," Maggie said, turning her attention from Heath to Tony, "you must be one of those Protective Order of Saint Benedict boys trying not to draw attention to themselves down in Lake Oswego. Is it true that you all go by 'brother' so your enemies can't tell who's a priest and who isn't?"

Maggie let the words hang, but Tony didn't look like he wanted to answer. Pity. Heath would have liked to hear that answer. Maggie gave him a different smile then, the kind she used when she thought she might need to take charge of a situation.

"You aren't here to cause me trouble, are you?"

"No," Tony said, grabbing a seat at the bar and taking a deep breath. He glanced at Drake with an encouraging nod before turning his attention back to Maggie. "I solemnly swear on the Blood of Christ that I come here tonight only to help bring peaceful solutions to a potentially deadly dispute."

"Fair enough." Maggie quirked an eyebrow. "And drink, I expect. This isn't a park, you know."

"Of course," Tony said with an embarrassed smile. Then he glanced up to look at his options and blinked his eyes wide.

No mirror behind the bar. Not at a place like Gripper. The last thing Maggie needed was some drunken fool using a big mirror to conjure something that she would then have to put back down. Instead she had six shelves of alcohols, from the cheapest bourbon anyone could talk themselves into swallowing to a smattering of Irish whiskeys so old that Mrs. Halloran's grandmother might have been on a first-name basis with them.

"Got a few more things that aren't on display," she said quietly. "Heath here can list them for you, or come close enough to give you a notion."

"Oh," Tony said, "I suspect you have an absinthe that would bring a few of the brothers here on a weekly basis, if your charming door-lady allowed them entry." He pointed to a bottle on the top shelf. "Is ... is that Griffin's Roost?"

"It is indeed," Maggie said, looking at Tony with a little more respect. "And that particular bottle was taken from a cask aged one hundred fifty years. As you might expect, it's a wee bit pricey."

"If this goes well, I'll buy a round of it for everyone currently seated at the bar, including the bartender."

"I ... I think that's my cue," Drake said. He had a high voice, a bit weak-sounding in Heath's opinion.

Heath turned to face Drake who stepped up next to him.

THE ENTIRE ROOM SEEMED TO HOLD ITS BREATH AS DRAKE STEPPED closer.

Drake and Heath stood not much more than arm's-length apart now, for perhaps the first time ever. Up close Heath could smell Drake's cheap dandruff shampoo, but he could also smell too much of a deodorant that was supposed to suggest the wearer was sporty and athletic.

In that moment, Heath felt pity for Drake. The poor bastard just seemed like an unhappy individual.

Nevertheless, Heath's hand was in his pocket and clutching the right packet of powders before he even thought about moving. Just a reaction to having Drake step within arm's reach. Just in case Drake tried to pull something.

Maggie cleared her throat. Loudly.

Heath eased his now-empty hand out of his pocket.

"Show 'em to me," Maggie said. Heath showed her both sides of his empty hands. She nodded, and slid his mostly full glass of Hef to him. "Give your hands something to do and let the man talk."

Heath picked up his beer, and Maggie spoke louder.

"I don't see anyone drinking."

Most of the room sipped or gulped something from their glasses then, including Vizinha, who held up her Manhattan in toast to Heath before she sipped from the rim.

"Quite a crowd, wouldn't you say?" Tony asked, rubbing his hands together as he stepped up like a referee between two boxers. Then he lowered his voice. "Ignore them, Mandrake. They must bear witness, but the only judgment you have to worry about is that of the Almighty."

Drake's eyes flicked to Tony, then to the floor. He rubbed his palms on the legs of his cargo pants, and had a few drops of sweat on his forehead and neck.

"Did you know he was my brother?" Drake asked.

Heath gave him a stone face. "You don't get to ask questions or play nice. Not until you've said what I came here to hear."

"Heath," Tony admonished, "there's no reason to be rude."

"I'm not the one who started this."

"Yes, you—" Drake stopped himself, swallowed hard, and turned back to the bar to pick up his own glass of some pale ale or other.

Heath waited while Drake drained a good quarter of the glass before setting his beer back down and wiping his mouth with the back of his hand.

"Doesn't matter," Drake said, as though to convince himself. He cleared his throat and wiped his forehead with the back of his arm. Then he turned to face the crowd, arms raised.

"Everybody," Drake said, "I need your attention."

He gave them a moment as though the room had to settle down, even though everyone was already hanging on the conversation at the bar.

"The other night," Drake said, "I condemned Heath Cyr to die, for interfering in my affairs. I hereby rescind, withdraw, and commute that condemnation. I also offer Heath Cyr my sincere apology for my efforts against him, and hope that this will prove sufficient to move him to cease his workings against myself and my family."

That last brought a murmur through the room. A murmur Heath didn't like at all.

"I never threatened his family," Heath said.

"Oh," Drake said, his high voice growing shrill. "But you *did*. You hit both me and my brother — *the priest* — with your *zombie powder*, but you were going to go ahead with your spells unless I offered my apology. Which I have."

"Now, wait just one damned second," Heath said.

"Your vendetta against me was fair," Drake continued, growing even louder. "After all, I wanted to kill you. But my brother? He committed no crime except visiting me in my hour of spiritual need."

The room was definitely abuzz now.

"Come *on*," Heath said, loud enough to be heard in the corners of the room and trying to ignore the smile on Mrs. Halloran's face, where she stood near the door. "Everyone here knows my reputation. I have never, *not once*, struck anyone but my intended target. And I had no reason to target anyone but Drake."

"But your back was against the wall, wasn't it, Twilight?" Drake was in full-on drama mode now, standing as straight as his posture could manage and pointing like he had the finger of doom. "You felt my demons closing in. You were willing to do anything to stop me, even if it meant taking down *an innocent man*."

"Oh, please," Heath said, trying to be heard over the louder buzz of conversation now. One advantage Drake's high voice gave him — it was more piercing than Heath's baritone. "I could have done anything to Drake I wanted and never given Tony here so much as a sweat."

A word from the monk here might have helped, but Tony stood slack-jawed and staring at his brother in disbelief.

Somewhere behind Heath, Colin wasn't saying a word. Heath had that back-of-the-neck kind of feeling that Colin was doing something, and trying very hard not to be noticed while he did it.

Meanwhile, Vizinha was smiling as though this were the most entertaining evening she could have imagined.

"So *you* say," Drake said. "But my brother's own fellows — the Protective Order of Saint Benedict — couldn't prove that. And they *considered* you an ally, of sorts."

"What are you doing?" Tony said, voice sharp. "How dare you tell anyone that—"

"I know for a fact," Drake continued, "that the head of their order visited Twilight earlier today, to beg clemency for Tony."

"That's a lie," Heath said, though he had the feeling that most of the room no longer cared about the truth. "I was visited by a monk today, but that monk already knew the truth — that Tony here was in no danger from me."

Drake was done. He turned and marched toward the door. The room buzzed even louder now. Mrs. Halloran watched Heath like a hawk, waiting for him to make a move against the exiting Drake.

Heath shook his head and forced himself to sip a little of his beer. It was every bit as cold and refreshing as it had been a minute or two ago, but just then Heath didn't find it refreshing at all.

"So," Maggie said to Tony, "I'm guessing you won't be buying a round of Griffin's Roost."

"No," Tony said. Poor guy looked as though he'd been gut-punched twice. "But I'll take a shot of bourbon. Appalachian Gold. A double."

MAGGIE JOINED THE MONK FOR THE BOURBON, THEN HAD HER HANDS full with all the drink orders that started coming in. Conversation was running in full-force at the Gripper now, and conversation was thirsty work.

Colin came up to sit on the stool beside Heath at the bar, with Tony on Heath's other side and Vizinha three seats farther down. The devil in red.

"I had no idea," Tony said, rolling his untasted glass back and forth between two fingers, sounding like a little kid who's been told Christmas was canceled. "I believed he was ready to repent his ways."

"Might've been," Heath said, trailing his finger through the sweat on his glass of beer. "But I think he played you. Played both of us." Heath jerked a thumb toward the roomful of occultists behind him. "Some will think it's gauche. Others will think it's wrong or bad karma. Some will just call it sloppy. But any of them that believe I'd've hurt you are going to look down on me for it."

Colin opened his mouth to say something, but closed it again and sipped his own beer.

"He did it well," Heath said, shaking his head with a touch of bitter admiration. "Just enough touches of truth to cast doubt and make me look bad. The ripples from this one won't go away quickly."

"No!" Tony slammed his fist on the bar, then slammed his bourbon like a seasoned drinker and thumped the glass back down. Fire in those brown eyes when he turned to Heath.

"They'll see the truth. I'll *make* them. I won't be the reason..."

Tony never finished that sentence. Just threw a twenty on the bar and started toward the nearest table like a boxer coming out of his corner.

"Hey, uh," Colin said quickly, "maybe I better go keep an eye on him. Just in case."

Colin scurried after the angry monk. And with Maggie dealing with drink orders, that meant the only two people still seated at the bar were Heath and Vizinha. The other patrons were giving them a wide berth.

"Well," Vizinha said, slipping up to sit beside Heath, and flashing lots of toned leg as she did. "That was exciting."

"What do you think?" Heath said, sipping his beer and hoping he wasn't about to get propositioned.

"The monk was never in any danger, of course. Even Dark Heath wouldn't get sloppy enough for collateral damage. But I approve of your approach. Frightened people make mistakes. Poor foolish Drake, for example, never asked for truce or armistice. He basically offered surrender without even *asking* you to let him off the hook."

She smiled like a fox in a henhouse.

"I'll bet you half of what those people are talking about is speculating whether or not you'll kill him anyway, for trying to embarrass you."

Heath got a sinking feeling in his gut. That conversation with Brother Theodopolis all too fresh in his mind.

"Is that what *you* think?" Heath's mouth was getting dry, but he couldn't quite bring himself to take another sip of his beer. "That I'd kill him for embarrassing me?"

"Well, face it," Vizinha said, leaning forward at just the right angle to show her cleavage to good advantage. Heath kept his gaze right on her eyes, which only widened her smile. "Your monk there isn't going to convince anybody of the truth. Especially not when he's still trying to hide his order."

She gave a throaty chuckle. "As though half the people good enough to drink here didn't know about them already."

"So you didn't coach Drake for tonight?" Heath stared hard into those chestnut eyes, trying to pierce whatever façade she kept up.

"Not I," she said, sipping her drink. "Oh, I know. When he comes here he looks like he lives in his mother's basement, eating pizza and trolling internet forums. Honestly, though, it's because he knows the women here aren't his type and the guys will be more impressed by his skills than his show. When he's out in the world he wears sharp outfits that make his weight work *for* him."

Heath made himself sip from his beer now, to avoid having to clear his throat. Too much happening tonight. Too much information coming too fast. Had the feeling he'd be processing all this for a while.

"So he doesn't have a crush on you?"

"Me?"

Vizinha laughed — really laughed — and Heath was suddenly aware again that she wasn't born in the United States. Yes, she still had traces of an accent, though she'd worked hard to develop an American style of speech. But her full-throated laughter had a wet quality about it. As though instead of a ha-ha-ha or he-he-he sound it dipped in the middle of each sound. Like hwe-hwe-hwe, bubbling out of her.

It wasn't good or bad, it was just ... unexpected. Real.

Smooth Portuguese followed for a few words, before she slipped back to English.

"Oh, that was a good one. No, *nego*, I'm way too much woman for him and he knows it. He likes his girls barely legal and ... pliant. Drake wants my allegiance, not my *boceta*. Not that he'd have a chance. Most often I prefer the fairer sex, but when it comes to men..." Her eyes roamed up and down Heath. "I like my playmates fit, and my men dark. In more ways than one."

"So poor Colin has no shot with you?"

Heath sipped a little more beer while Vizinha turned to regard Colin, trailing along behind Tony's vain attempt to disseminate actual facts.

"I like that he uses weird magic that shouldn't work. And that he's openly bisexual. But to me, only a girl can be that pale, thin and blond and get my motor going." She turned her smile back to Heath. "But let's talk about you."

"You *do* know I'm dating Nariko."

"Please." Vizinha waved a dismissive hand. "She's a momma's girl with anger issues. You need a real woman. A woman who understands your magic, as well as your needs."

"A woman who tried to kill me not too long ago?"

"Ancient history," she said with another dismissive wave. "Besides, I didn't want to kill you. I wanted to make you *wish* you were dead. Huge difference."

Heath couldn't help a snort of laughter at that. Here this woman was trying to be sexy and she stumbled onto almost the exact same phrasing his uncle Andre would have used. Uncle Andre would have said "big difference," instead of "huge" but otherwise...

Heath finished his beer, and as he did, Vizinha's posture shifted. Got straighter. Less flirty and more businesslike.

She sighed through her nose.

"You aren't Dark Heath at all, are you?" she asked. "It was just an act. You're still trying to be a white-light-goody-goody."

"Can't even say that," Heath said, tossing a five down on the bar for his beer. "I guess I'm just what they call me. Twilight."

11

———

FOR THE FIRST TIME HEATH COULD REMEMBER, MRS. HALLORAN DIDN'T give him a hard time before handing over his backpack. But then, Heath figured her smile said everything she wanted it to say anyway.

Heath didn't let her close the door on him, though. Not right away. He stayed just inside the doorway — and just inside Gripper's wards — while he looked over the street.

Drake was still out there, and he had a pair of demons with him. Little things, barely enough power to cause a heat ripple in the dimming light of the setting sun, sitting on Drake's shoulders. Familiars, no doubt. Gifts from some conjured major demon or other, and forced to wait outside while he did his drinking.

The way Drake's head was moving, he was looking for something. Something he expected to be tucked away in someone's car, or...

Or he was looking for Heath's car.

"Don't tell me you're afraid of that pasty doughboy," Mrs. Halloran said through scorn thick enough to clog a sewer pipe. "Go on, get, if you're going. If you're done drinking you don't get to hide behind my skirts."

Gripper's wards were cast by Maggie, not Mrs. Halloran, but pointing that out wouldn't have done Heath any kindnesses. So he stepped outside the wards and onto the sidewalk. A moment later Drake looked up.

Their eyes met, and Drake's widened.

Heath smiled. He was too jumbled up inside to feel as confident as he looked, but appearances counted for plenty more than Drake seemed to think. Even among practitioners.

Heath started walking Drake's direction.

"I have four demons with me," Drake said, "and—"

"You have those two little pissants," Heath said, "but that's it." He kept his pace even as he walked, but he kept talking so Drake couldn't rally through conversation.

"Now I've face down a marquis and a president, both of your own workings. And I'm still here. So you tell me now, just what do you think the chances are that those tiny little specks that pass for your familiars can doing anything to me that I don't myself feel inclined to let them do?"

Heath stopped walking just outside of arm's reach.

"Well?"

Heath dropped the smile.

"Hey," Drake said, his hands coming up like he was surrendering, even though one of them held an open pocketknife. Only about three inches long, it had a wooden handle, stained black, and a steel blade dinged and scuffed from many years of use. "I just beat you at your own game, that's—"

Drake noticed Heath staring at the knife. Dropped the knife.

"That wasn't for you," Drake said quickly. "That was—"

"What?" Heath said, voice flat. "Gonna slash my tire, but you can't find my car?"

Drake flushed.

"Really?" Heath blinked, then laughed, which made Drake flush all the brighter. "Big bad karcist wants to slash my tires?"

Embarrassment melted out of Drake's eyes now, replaced by anger. He drew a deep breath to make some pronouncement or other, but Heath spoke first.

"I didn't say you could talk. Swear to God you are on my last nerve. In fact, maybe I should just—"

"Heath!"

Tony's voice. Of course. Then those had to be Tony's shoes slapping the asphalt as he hot-footed it across the street. Heath reached up and rubbed the bridge of his nose. Laying some smack down on Drake right now might just smooth out all the rough edges inside Heath and give him room to think. But the Lwa were laughing again, because Heath wasn't even going to get to do that.

"I know the feeling," Drake said.

"Don't do it, Heath," Tony said, coming to a halt not quite between Heath and Drake. The big monk didn't even have the grace to sound winded after his sprint. "I know my brother was about to do something stupid, and I know he's done plenty to earn your wrath, but I'm begging you. Just—"

"Baal's blood, Mark," said Drake, "would you just *shut the fuck up*?"

Heath blinked for a moment, making sure in his own mind that Drake just called Tony "Mark."

Tony didn't seem to notice. He bent down and picked up the pocketknife. Meanwhile, Drake kept at him.

"You're not my fucking keeper, and my soul is none of your damned business."

Tony was standing now, making a show of closing the knife, but the way he looked at it told Heath he recognized the knife. That Drake'd had it for a very long time, and Tony didn't always approve of how Drake used it.

"I'll take that," Heath said, snatching the knife out of Tony's hand.

"No!" Drake said.

"You know what, *Shawn Aaron Martinson*," Tony said to Drake, "maybe I should just let Heath here have the knife along with your birth name. You want to play the big bad Satanist? Or karcist? Or whatever you call what you do? You want to abuse your own brother's love and trust to further your own ends? Maybe you deserve whatever Heath decides to do to you."

"*He* was using you too," Drake said, the petulant baby brother.

"I didn't leave him much choice," Tony said, eyes flicking to Heath before he turned to step between Heath and Drake. "But you, you're my *brother*. That's supposed to *mean* something."

Heath knew better than to bear witness to a family squabble. If he stayed, sooner or later they'd turn on him as the interloper. So he turned and walked back across the street toward his car.

Besides, Heath had managed to come out ahead after all. He now had a knife that had clearly been Drake's for a long time and seen a lot of use. Or rather, Heath now had *Shawn Aaron Martinson's* knife, which might be even better.

Just Heath's having that knife would probably be enough to keep Drake from getting obnoxious. And if not, well, maybe Heath would do a litmus test on the value of a true birth name over a well-identified nickname, when combined with a solid link...

"Heath," said Colin, hustling out of the bar. He had a worried look on his face, but seeing Tony and Drake going at each other in furtive voices across the street seemed to ease out some of his tension.

"Good," Colin said with a sigh. "Tony said something bad was about to happen, but I still had to pay for my beer. Oh!" He pulled a five out of his pocket. "Maggie said your beer was on her."

Heath chuckled and tucked the bill in his pocket.

"Have to remember to thank her," he said, "but right now I want to get the hell out of here."

"Want a ride?"

Heath smiled. They were standing right next to the *Parakeet* and even Colin couldn't notice it.

"No thanks," Heath said, pulling out his car keys. "Got it right here."

Colin didn't seem to twig to the situation until Heath was opening his driver's side door.

"Holy crap," Colin said. "That piece of junk is *yours*?"

"Watch it," Heath said, slinging his backpack into the passenger seat. "You're not nearly so cute as Nariko."

HEATH HAD GOTTEN ONLY ABOUT FOUR BLOCKS BY SIDE STREETS, HALF-formed plan coming together in his mind, when he started swearing and pulled over.

Timing could be everything. Vizinha would only stay at Gripper so long, even if she wanted to see how the rumor mill played out. She might even leave early, if she suspected Heath might move against her. He didn't have much to spare for arguments and backtalk.

But he had promised not to cut his friends out of his plans. And he was going to stick to that promise. He was not going to walk the solitary path of Uncle Andre. Especially if Brother Theodopolis was right and Heath was already getting a little too comfortable on the darker side of *gris-gris*.

So Heath sighed, picked up his phone, and called Colin.

"Look at the light," Colin said, by way of greeting.

Heath looked first at the stoplight a couple blocks farther down the street, then back at the stoplight he'd just pulled through.

Colin waved from the driver's seat of his Saturn, sitting at the red light. Colin wasn't holding a phone, but then, Colin had a Bluetooth setup. While the *Parakeet* had many virtues, supporting hands-free calling wasn't one of them.

"Had the feeling you might be up to something," Colin said. Heath shook his head and hung up. The light changed and Colin pulled up next to where Heath was parked. Eased down his window, but Heath's was still up. Colin mouthed, "Want a lift?"

Heath snorted a laugh, but hopped out of his car, locked it, and jumped into the passenger seat of Colin's Saturn.

"We need to find out where Vizinha lives—"

"Already know," Colin said. When Heath's eyebrows climbed high enough to plant a flag atop his skull, Colin snickered. "She doesn't care if people knows she lives behind her shop."

"And you know where that is?"

"Honestly," Colin said, "you need to get over to the east side more often. No idea how much you're missing."

Heath made two quick phone calls while Colin drove. More deciduous trees on the east side, and fewer of the Douglas firs and pines than Heath's own neighborhood — not to mention vastly more grassy lawns — but it was pretty, in its way. Less like buildings growing in a forest than a suburb that just happened to be part of the city itself.

But then, so far Colin had been staying away from major streets, paralleling the diagonal thoroughfare Sandy Boulevard before cutting south down 32nd. Odd mix of new and old construction as they steered into Laurelhurst. Some buildings were decades old, but others had been built or refurbished within the last few years.

One of those neighborhoods that was nice, but not too nice. Solid client base for Vizinha, because the people living nearby had money, but not so much they could just throw money at *everything* they wanted in life. The kind of people who could buy expensive spells.

In other words, a higher class of clientele than Heath tended to attract.

Colin parked across the street from *Botanica da Nosso Senhora*, a small shop with seven-day candles and statues of saints in the front window. The shop's name was done in vivid red lettering on the glass. Over the roof, Heath could see the lot extended to include a two-story house in back.

The street was modestly busy for a Friday night, mostly people driving through the neighborhood on their way to food or entertainment. A handful of middle-aged pedestrians looked like a group bound for the antique shop at the end of the block. They had the laughing posture of people who'd enjoyed wine with their dinner.

Cleaner smell to the neighborhood here, than over by Gripper. Freshened by the trees and the grass of the residences on the surrounding blocks, and helped by the fact that nearby Stark wasn't nearly so busy as Burnside.

"Nice setup," Heath said. "Storefront of her own. No hustling clients, and if she can handle the rent and utilities and still make enough to keep her in fancy dresses, she must be doing pretty well."

"Maybe Nariko's right about your rates?" Colin had the grace to sound embarrassed.

"Maybe." Heath glanced up and down the street, but no sign of the others yet. "Then again, Vizinha offers services I wouldn't touch."

Colin snickered, but Colin could spot a double-entendre at fifty yards on a cloudy day. Heath had long since learned to ignore those moments.

The sun was finally vanishing into twilight when a black Mercedes pulled up behind them, Hershel at the wheel. Hershel immediately got out of the car, wearing a smoke gray suit. In the time it took him to shoot his cuffs, Hershel looked to have gotten a read on the whole neighborhood.

"Unlock the back," Heath said, as Goldilocks got out of the Mercedes.

Goldilocks was a short-haired redhead this time, standing not much over five feet tall. She had large breasts that strained a pink v-necked tee shirt, and painted-on bell bottom jeans that tapered to some impressive curves on a small-waisted frame. She wore heels high enough that as she walked her hips swayed like concert lighters during a meaningful song.

Colin was practically drooling, and didn't seem to realize his mouth was hanging open.

"Back," Colin said, unlocking all four doors with the push of a button on his center console. "Get in the back. The lady rides up front."

"We're not going anywhere," Heath said.

"Back."

Heath sighed, snatched up his backpack, and hopped out of the front seat and into the back before Colin went into conniptions. As he moved, Heath glanced to see where Hershel was, but the Bodyguard seemed to have vanished.

Goldilocks smiled as she passed Heath, and slid into the seat he'd vacated.

"Good evening, boys," she said, smile widening then vanishing as she shook her head.

"Hi," Colin said in what was probably supposed to be a sexy tone. "I'm Colin."

He held out his hand, but Goldilocks put her fingers to her furrowed brow.

"Don't touch me," she said quickly.

"I'm sorry," Colin said, just as fast. "I didn't mean—"

Heath reached out and clamped a hand over Colin's mouth to stop what would have been a nervous flow of chatter. Meanwhile, Goldilocks didn't seem to breathe, which might have been good for Colin, whose eyes were gorging themselves on her as it was.

Finally, she pulled her fingers down. Blinked her eyes rapidly, then smirked at Colin.

"You're a randy one, aren't you?"

Colin started licking Heath's hand, and Heath yanked his hand away and wiped it on the back of Colin's seat.

"So that's the look of Colin's ideal woman?" Heath asked before Colin could speak again.

"Oh yes," she said, "and he has definite ideas about personality. Hard not to play to them."

"But I love all women," Colin said, a touch defensive.

"Yes, you do," Goldilocks said, "but deep inside, maybe even deeper than you admit to, this is the look and style you want most in a woman."

"Guilty as charged," Colin said, flushing the current color of her hair. "What's my sentence?"

"Stop," Heath and Goldilocks said at the same time.

"You need to cool it," Heath said. "We need her on point, not on *your* point."

"Nice one," Colin said. "For you, I mean."

"He's nearby," Goldilocks said, going straight to the reason they were here — her male counterpart. "I think."

"You can't be sure?" Heath asked. "I mean, there's a real chance that she stashed him somewhere. Motel maybe."

"No," Goldilocks said, fingers to her forehead again. "Vizinha couldn't risk leaving him where a woman or a gay man might find him ... I *think* he's nearby. I can *almost* feel him, but not quite."

"Must be Vizinha's wards," Colin said, leaning forward as though trying to make the moment intimate. "Don't worry. I can bring them down."

"Do I have to turn the hose on you?" Heath said.

"He'd just enjoy it," Goldilocks said.

Heath pulled a packet from his pocket and blew a handful of red pepper, black cat hair — and a couple of other things — in Colin's face.

Colin sneezed. Shook his head. Rubbed his eyes. Looked at Goldilocks like he was puzzled, then his eyes got wider than his steering wheel. His hand darted between his legs.

"Don't worry," Heath said. "It's temporary. Just so you can focus."

"This is so not cool." Colin shook his head. "*So* not cool. I—"

"I will slap your face," Heath said. "Pull it together. Tony can only keep Vizinha at Gripper so long without it looking suspicious, and I can't do this if I have to keep you from humping my client's leg."

The image got a snicker out of Colin, but then he said, "Long as you promise this is temporary. They don't call me Mr. Eveready for nothing."

Heath almost — *almost* — asked Colin who called him that. But decided he'd rather not know.

"I promise," Heath said. "By dawn you'll be your normal horny self. But right now, you're on street duty. Keep anyone from noticing anything odd, and if Vizinha gets back, either warn me or delay her or both."

"But—"

"There's no need for that," Goldilocks said. "Hershel will handle street duty."

"I thought your bodyguard needed to be by your side."

"Trust me. If I'm threatened, you'll find out what 'bodyguard' means. In the meantime, Hershel can't help with the infiltration, but giving us a warning, that he can do."

Heath looked back and forth between Goldilocks and Colin.

Bringing them along meant putting them both in harm's way, which Heath didn't like at all. But they wanted to be there, and Heath had to admit, he might need their help.

He forced a lopsided smile onto his face.

"Let's go."

BY THE TIME THE THREE OF THEM WERE HALFWAY ACROSS THE STREET, Goldilocks looked once more the way Heath had first seen her. A generically beautiful blond with a figure that was nice, but not too nice. Like someone who should have been starring in an evening soap opera or something. Her only concession to their situation was having her hair back in a ponytail, and wearing a black, skintight jumpsuit like some kind of special ops agent or something.

Colin jumped at the transformation, but then, he hadn't seen it before. Didn't comment though. Maybe he was learning.

The three of them stopped at the front window of *Botanica da Nossa Senhora*, as though they were potential customers admiring the saints statues.

"Any better sense yet?" Heath asked Goldilocks.

"I can feel that he's nearby," she said, frustration in her words. "That's all." She shivered. "I've never felt cut off from him for so long. I feel ... hollow."

Colin put a hand on her shoulder, and it looked more like a compassionate gesture than a sexual one, so Heath figured his little powder was still doing its job.

But the easy part was over. They were now just outside Vizinha's property and her wards. The former was just as dangerous as the latter, in some ways. Heath had been good about staying clear of legal troubles in part because he tried to avoid doing things like trespassing, breaking-and-entering, and so forth.

"The lock's a joke," Colin said. "When we're ready I can pick it in under twenty seconds or I'll buy you both lunch tomorrow."

Suddenly Heath remembered Colin's offhand comments about arrests but no convictions.

"What about mundane alarms?" Goldilocks asked.

"She wouldn't," Heath said. "What message would it send her customers if she needed mundane help to protect her business."

"I don't see any stickers," Colin said, "but you know what they say. Trust in Allah, but tie up your camel."

"Fine, you check on those while I take a close look for spirits."

Heath opened his spirit eyes.

Feeling the wards had been easy enough, but now he could really see them. Like smooth, violet fog that reached the edge of the sidewalk but came no further. Within them he could pick out all the details he'd mentioned, but now a few more. Little compulsions. Complex things that checked each person who entered to see if they had any juju, and if not, they'd tend to find Vizinha's wares just a little prettier than they were. A little more fascinating. More like the kinds of things they wanted to have. And more than that, that any candles she'd dressed or spell bags — Heath refused to call what she made conjure hands or mojo bags — were certain to do what they said.

Cheating. Heath tutted in his head.

Then Heath spotted them. A half-dozen watchdog spirits, waiting inside the shop. Dormant right now, but there was a thread — a tiny wisp of ward — that would wake them up the moment anybody entered when the shop was closed.

The spirits were nasty looking things. Like piranhas that swam through the air, but they dined on motivation, drive, willpower. Each one looked as though it could vegetate a man's spirit in twenty seconds flat.

Heath whistled disturbed admiration.

"Found the spirits," he said.

"Found the alarm," Colin said, triumphant. "Silent and wireless. Not sure it goes to a company or something private. Got a ward to alert her if it gets disabled. It alerts something else too. Probably those watchdogs."

"She's thorough," Goldilocks said. "No wonder she caught him."

Heath made the mistake of turning to look at her with his spirit eyes open.

Perfection.

Absolute perfection. Beyond the beauty any mere mortal could manage. Head to toe, every inch of the woman in front of him overflowed with sexuality. Her skin was all tones, shifting as though glimmering, and every tone desirable. Not a stitch of clothing covered her, and the magnificence of her face and figure brought tears to Heath's eyes and dropped him to his knees.

And her scent, like honey and orange blossoms that had been in the air when Heath was thirteen and falling in love for the first time with Darla Hopkins from down the street. Only this time the honey and orange blossom scent was purer, stronger. And there was something underlying it that Heath couldn't quite pick out, but that went right to his spinal column and made him shiver.

He would worship this woman. He would do anything for her. If only she would deign to share that perfection with him. Even once.

His cargo shorts were terribly uncomfortable, but it was the best kind of uncomfortable. And if she saw, if she — She — knew, She might take pity on him and grant him release. He needed only speak Her name. Her True name, which was even now on the tip of his tongue.

His mouth was dry. Nerves. Of course he was nervous before such a goddess. Still, even if Her name came out choked, it would be enough. Enough to get Her attention. The rest would...

Smack!

A slap, from a Creole woman's hand. A flash of pink dress and perfume. Florida water.

Heath was still on his knees there on the sidewalk, but now his spirit eyes were closed. Goldilocks stood before him, brow furrowed with worry, but she looked only TV-beautiful once again. Not the irresistible gloriousness of a moment before. And she was back in her black jumpsuit.

Colin was calling Heath's name, over and over.

Heath shook his head. Held up his hands. "I'm all right now. I'm all right."

That was and was not a lie. He might not be all right for a while, not after seeing that. But he felt more together than he probably should have, after what he just saw. Probably a side benefit to that slap.

He puffed out a deep sigh.

"You looked at me with magical sight," Goldilocks said, "when I wasn't ready for it. I would advise against that."

"Yeah," Heath said, standing up. "Figured that out." He nodded at Colin, who looked as though he thought Heath needed a trip to the emergency room. "You don't do it either. No magical eyes on her."

Colin nodded, but didn't look any more relaxed. Just how bad did Heath look?

"Someone saved you," Goldilocks said. "Was it—"

"Ezili Freda Dahomey," Heath said. "Lwa of love, and jealousy. Not going to speculate which aspect made her decide to help."

Heath wondered, and not for the first time, just exactly how many Lwa were watching him. And what they wanted with him, for that matter.

Although, in this case, he had to admit he was glad for the help.

"Clock's ticking," Colin said.

"Right." Heath turned back to examine the wards and spirits again.

But his spirit eyes wouldn't open.

Heath stood there on the sidewalk outside Vizinha's store, between Colin and Goldilocks. Heath's back was tight, waist to shoulders, and he'd scraped his knees dropping to them on the rough sidewalk.

But those were only details beside the worst part.

"Fuck," Heath said. "Looks like Ezili slammed my spirit eyes shut tight for a while."

"Why?" Colin asked.

"Might not have meant to." Heath sighed. "I've got Ghede Brav's flask in my pocket, and Ezili and the Ghedes … don't get along."

"Never mind that," Goldilocks said. "About your spirit eyes. How bad is this?"

"Bad," said Colin. "But hey, you're not alone, Heath. You're just going to have to follow my lead for a change. I'll handle the alarm, while you do something about those nasties."

"Wait," Heath said. "We're going about this wrong. There's no way she's keeping Mr. Perfect in her shop."

"Mr. Perfect?" Goldilocks asked, one eyebrow high as though she weren't sure how she felt about that name for her counterpart.

"Colin's name for him, but it'll work better than anything else. Otherwise I'll end up calling him Papa Bear or something."

Heath shook his head.

"Doesn't matter anyway. No way she could keep an avatar of sex that close at hand without … sampling the goods. Especially if she's looked at him they way I looked at Goldilocks here. And Vizinha doesn't strike me as the type to tryst in the back room of her shop."

"You're thinking her house?" Colin asked.

"Attic or basement. Unless she actually keeps him chained to her bed or something."

"If she's using him for magic though," Goldilocks said, "would those places work?"

Heath nodded. "People like us can work anywhere."

"Not 'like us,'" Colin said. "You're nothing like her, Heath."

"I'm starting to think I'm more like her than I want to be."

"Heath—"

"Incoming," Hershel said, just popping right out of the air next to Goldilocks and interrupting whatever Colin was going to say next.

Heath looked up to the end of the street, where a metallic blue Dodge Viper rumbled down the block slowly enough to make its rumble a sound of impending doom.

Heath watched it approach. No point in trying to hide or look innocent. Not now.

The Viper halted in front of them, but the rumble of its engine made it look as though it were still in motion. The spin of its rims helped the illusion.

The tinted passenger window scrolled down. Vizinha smiled at them from the driver's seat.

"I'm not late, am I?" she said. "Monks can be so charming when they're trying not to be offensive. Almost like they're real people."

"No," Heath said, trying to pick up her game while he figured out a new angle. "We only just got here ourselves, and were admiring your statues. I particularly like the Saint Expedite. Very natural looking."

"I'll give you one on the house," she said. "Just let me put Baby away. I'll meet you all in back."

Vizinha rumbled her car into the driveway and past her shop. The license plate said simply A MAE.

"Of course she calls it 'baby,'" Colin said.

"The mother?" Goldilocks asked, translating the license plate. "You said something about that before."

"As in mother of saints. It's a title in Umbanda and Quimbanda. Hell, Candomblé too, far as I know. She's saying she's not just any *mãe-de-santo*, but *the mãe-de-santo*. The biggest and baddest, or whatever."

"This is a trap," Hershel said, making Heath jump. He'd forgotten the bodyguard was there. For a great big guy in a smoke gray suit, Hershel had done an admirable job of blending into the background.

"No way we should follow her," Hershel said, words entirely for Goldilocks. "You're paying Heath to do a job. Let him do it and let me get you someplace safe."

"I can't," Goldilocks said. "Not when we're so close."

"He's right," Heath said. "You're the client. You shouldn't be in harm's way, not with Vizinha here. Colin and I can handle this. And if we can't, the last thing we should do is hand you over to her."

"But—" Goldilocks said.

"You're paying for the man's advice, as much as his skill," Hershel said. "Listen to him, if you won't listen to me."

"Fine!" Goldilocks snapped. "Bring the car."

"Come on," Heath said, leading Colin toward the driveway and the back of the house before Goldilocks could change her mind and tag along.

"We're giving up the best distraction we could ask for," Colin said, falling into step next to Heath while, behind them, Goldilocks protested the whole way to her car. "Losing her could make the difference, you know."

"And you know Hershel's right," Heath said. "This is a trap. Bringing her with us would be irresponsible, at best."

"Why are we walking into a trap again?" Colin asked. "Why are we doing this now, instead of waiting for Nariko, aka, backup?"

"We're not waiting for Nariko," Heath said, "because this is already in motion, and some things, once in motion, need to finish. And as for backup..."

Heath looked up to see a powder blue Subaru Forester zoom around the corner and up to the curb, Tony at the wheel.

"He's here."

Tony hopped out of his car and hustled up to Heath and Colin. The monk looked a little worn and bedraggled from the evening's events, and he threw an obviously dead cell phone onto the sidewalk.

"Vizinha shut it down on you?" Colin said, not entirely keeping the surprise out of his voice. Colin knew, as Heath did, that Tony should have kept that from happening.

"I was ready for her to try and I still didn't even catch her doing it." Tony shook his head. "I'm sorry. I was too distracted by Sean. Twice a fool in one night."

That might have worried Heath, except that Tony didn't look like a fool. He looked big, and angry, and the determination in his eye was a force of its own.

But Heath had to be sure. Had to know the monk was ready for what they were about to do. He raised an eyebrow.

Tony gave a grimly determined nod.

Good enough.

"Let's go," Heath said.

12

HEATH LED AS THE TRIO WALKED AROUND THE SIDE OF THE SMALL SHOP and down the smooth, paved driveway. Not long after dusk, and the gray, darkening air still carried some of the day's warmth, but the night birds were already singing.

Colin and Tony followed a step behind Heath, forming a wedge that might have looked dramatic and badass in slow motion.

Heath didn't feel too dramatic at the moment though. His stomach felt as though a fleet of ferrets were running wild, and his knees still felt shaky from the sight of Goldilocks' true form. He'd done a decent job of playing it off — and he had the feeling that Ezili had minimized the impact — but he suspected that the sight and smell of Goldilocks' true form would haunt him for some time.

Worse, *that* was what Vizinha was fighting for. She had the male equivalent of what Heath had seen, had *named* even if he tried to not even think that name. No doubt Vizinha'd fight harder than ever to keep what she had, no matter what the consequences to the greater populace.

And she'd already beaten Heath once, without such motivations.

So Heath tried to keep his pace steady down the driveway, and tried to convince himself that this wasn't a fool's errand. That he wasn't walking into an inescapable trap.

To remind himself that everyone is human. Everyone makes mistakes. He'd made one, looking at Goldilocks' true form. So Vizinha, she had to have made mistakes too.

Heath just needed to hold on long enough to find hers and exploit it.

The house in back was picturesque, even in the sudden brightness of the motion-sensor floodlights. Whitewashed two-story with picture windows and its own white picket fence. Yellow trim. Black tile roof that looked new. Well-tended garden in front. No growing herbs in pots on her back porch for Vizinha.

The garage at the end of the driveway matched the house, down to the new tiling on the roof.

"Wards?" Heath asked, and cursed inside that he had to ask. Right now his spirit eyes were shut so tight, he couldn't be sure what, if anything, he was really picking up.

"The wards on the shop cling to the shop," Colin said, softly. "Up ahead, the kind of *nothing-here* wards you might use, protecting her garage. The house ... too complicated to pick apart from here. Serious watchdog spirits behind those wards. I can tell that much."

Tony's eyes widened that Heath had to ask about wards, but he didn't question it.

As they rounded the corner of the shop, a step-stone path led to the fence gate. Heath could see the porch now, and it looked disturbingly similar to Heath's, in layout.

Exactly two chairs, with a table between them. Hers weren't cheap plastic though. They looked like some fine, orange hardwood.

Vizinha sat on one of the chairs, waiting. On another woman, the red chiffon dress might have looked too fancy for the simple setting, but Vizinha made it chic and casual at the same time.

"Where's the girl?" Vizinha asked. "I liked her *Mission Impossible* vibe. She was holding back, of course, but even that look worked on her. Remember what I was saying about pale blondes?"

"I remember," Heath said, coming to a stop just outside the gate.

He could feel her guardian spirits, ready to strike when she gave the command.

"Wards start at the gate," Colin muttered. "Watchdogs chomping at the bit."

"Problem is," Heath continued as though Colin hadn't spoken, "she wasn't along to be your date. She's looking for someone. A guy. Thought you might have seen him."

"Oh, *nego*, I've done more than see him." Vizinha's tone left no doubt about her meaning. "But if you're expecting me to give him up, you must have something to trade. And if it's not the girl..."

Vizinha's eyes roamed up and down Heath.

"You know that's not happening," Heath said. "Whether or not you approve of Nariko, she's still my girl and I'm still her man."

"Spoken like a man who's never been with a *brasileira*. One night with me and you'll forget all about your Japanese bitch."

The ferrets in Heath's stomach stilled. Something cold washed over him, and he let it infect his voice.

"Do not insult Nariko in my presence."

Vizinha sighed, then grimaced as she came to her feet. "Don't tell me you're in love with her." She shook her head. "No. That must be it. You haven't even noticed my legs or tried to look down my dress once, have you? Even your monk friend couldn't resist that."

Tony reddened. "The sins of the flesh call to all men. The vows of my order give me no special protection from them."

"*I* noticed," Colin grumbled, "but apparently I don't count."

"Enough of this game," Heath said, sweeping out his arms as though he could cut short the conversation with a gesture. "You knew you weren't going to seduce me. You're smarter than that. You probably don't even want to, and even if you did, you know that's not why I'm here."

"No," Vizinha said as though the whole conversation now bored her. "You thought you were going to break into my home and steal away a spirit I captured all on my own. And here I thought *you* were smarter than *that*."

"You know the consequences of binding one of these American Ideals, don't you? What will happen if he isn't freed?"

"I know what he claimed, but he'll say anything for his freedom, *não é*?" Vizinha cocked an eyebrow. "You believed that line of *lixo*?"

Heath didn't know what lee-shoo was, but he could make a pretty good guess from the way she said it. Before he could speak though, she started laughing again, that odd dipping sound.

"You did! Oh, *nego*, you're precious. I want to bottle you up and sell you."

"Right," Heath said, and the word came out clipped with anger. "Expecting you to be reasonable was stupid. I get that. So what's it going to be then? A deal or a duel?"

"Hmmm," Vizinha said, drawing out the word and tapping her chin with one finger as though she were torn between flavors of ice cream.

"If I have a choice," she said at last, "I pick neither. I beat you once, Heath, and I've learned a few things since then. You want to try to come at me? Here? Now?"

Her smile was cruel arrogance. She made bring-it-on gestures with both hands.

"Try it," she said.

"Heath does not stand alone," Tony bellowed, pointing one finger like Saint Peter condemning a soul to Hell. "Free your prisoner or in the name of Saint Marron you will face the consequences."

"Yeah," Colin said, jutting his jaw forward aggressively.

Vizinha shook her head, turned, and reached for her doorknob.

Tony reached both hands heavenward, and pulled a great big freaking sword out of midair. The blade blazed with golden fire.

Tony swung the sword in a single cut straight down to the ground.

Physically, he cleaved the little white front gate in two.

Magically, he sliced through all of Vizinha's carefully wrought wards in a single stroke. They shattered so fast that Heath's ears popped.

Vizinha whirled around, fire in her eyes.

Colin cracked his knuckles. "We'll handle the watchdogs. Take that bitch down."

Heath smiled.

WHEN HEATH LATER REMEMBERED THOSE MINUTES AFTER TONY SPLIT Vizinha's wards, he'd wonder how much of it really happened. Surely some of it had to have been his own imagination, fueled by closed spirit eyes and his desperate battle with Vizinha.

Vizinha in her red dress, face furious and hands almost crackling with power, walking slowly down the three steps of her front porch.

Tony to Heath's left, leaping and twirling like some hero out of Tolkien. His huge freaking sword burning with golden fire as he did battle with things Heath couldn't quite see.

Colin to Heath's right, chanting pseudo-Latin nonstop while his fingers worked a contraption that probably had a ridiculous name like Frater Magnifico's Superior Spirit Generator or something. Heath would have called it a "cootie catcher" because that's what the kids all called them when he was in grade school. Some kind of re-purposed origami fortune teller thing.

Still, Heath could feel it's power, and he could feel Colin calling spirits out of it faster than Heath would have believed. But then, Heath had never actually *seen* Colin fight before.

Unfortunately, he didn't have time to watch him now, because Vizinha was focused entirely on Heath's own self.

Heath locked eyes with her. Pushed that contact hard enough to start the *compelling gaze*. Fond as Vizinha was of making guys look at her legs or her chest, Heath figured she wouldn't have much experience with *compelling gaze*, if she even knew how to do it at all. There was always a chance he might even catch her off-guard and force her to surrender right away.

But Heath wasn't that lucky.

Both of them jarred as their wills collided.

The world narrowed down to her eyes and his. Couldn't have seen anything else around him if he wanted to. Just a long black tunnel connecting their eyes.

That wasn't normal. Normally the wills hit, one will yields, and that's about that. Oh, it might even take a moment or two, but not much more.

But in this case, neither will intended to go anywhere but through. Vizinha might not have had any particular experience with the *compelling gaze*, but she didn't get to be who she was without having a fair amount of willpower. What was more, she had a ton of anger backing her up.

That was all right. Heath had more than a little anger and frustration of his own pent up, and she made just as good an outlet for it as any. Hell, she was the source of a great deal of it. He focused everything into one command: surrender.

The pressure began to build between them. Not much more than a twinge at first, but then it continued.

Sharpened into a headache.

The ache spread to all the bones in his face and every single one of his teeth. Even to his tongue and lips.

Heath pushed harder. Thought about the dismissive, insulting way Vizinha talked about Nariko. *His* Nariko.

Either his teeth were grinding or he was growling now, but either way Heath just pushed at Vizinha all the harder.

And he felt her will start to give ground. He was right. She'd never learned *compelling gaze*. He could almost reach her mind. Heath doubled down. Strained with every part of himself to push that one insistent thought into her head: *surrender!*

But before it could take, she whistled a trill of sharp notes.

Their wills scraped against each other, burning like flint and steel as their contact broke. Fiery pain all the way through Heath's core. He couldn't stop the scream that came out of him. Only consolation was the matching scream that came out of Vizinha.

Heath was on his knees on the cobblestones of her garden path. Blinking. Nose bleeding. Tears trickling. Rushing sound in his ears. Pain flaring from every nerve in his body. He smelled burnt copper.

But some basic reflex, some nerve impulse so developed through habit that it never needed his brain to act, already had his hands in the pockets of his cargo shorts.

Maybe a dozen paces away, Vizinha. On her knees at the base of her steps. The bottom of her dress torn and dirty. She bled from her nose, her ears, her eyes.

"*Cú,*" she panted. "*Filho da puta ... Vou ...* I'm going to kill you for that."

She reached into her cleavage for a packet of powders. Heath could feel the power she gathered as she did. And it was no small amount of power. Way more than Heath could have called just then. Felt like everything she had. Not just her, herself, but calling on whatever she had built up inside her house. Every little trinket and fetish, spirit and ghostie — not to mention anything her *Orixás* were willing to lend in support — she was bringing together everything she had to make good on her threat.

Heath was already moving. Pulled a packet from his pocket. Tore the edge like the pin of a grenade and flung it right toward her face. Goofer dust, barberries and black hen feathers, asafetida, agrimony, Cruel Man of the Woods, flax, and a couple of things he'd been saving for a rainy day.

All prepped and flying through the air at her.

As he threw, Heath tried to pray. His tongue wasn't working right though. He couldn't do more than mouth words from Leviticus, and hope that whatever saints and Lwa kept an eye on him would carry his need to the Almighty.

"I then will destroy your high places, and cut down your incense altars, and heap your remains on the remains of your idols, for My soul shall abhor you."

She had her packet ready to throw when Heath's packet bomb hit her in the face, fully supported by whatever power Heath had left. More than that, it was supported by his prayer and his faith.

And all the power she raised broke. Like a great big water balloon, burst before she could throw it.

The air sizzled and flashed orange as directionless power flared out.

Heath's body didn't want to move, but he didn't give it any choice. He stumbled across the cobblestones to Vizinha.

She looked as shaky as he felt. Held up her hands like claws ready to scratch if he came close enough.

Heath stood just out of reach, swaying slightly. Knees shaking. Stomach roiling between hunger and never wanting to eat again.

He held up a length of green twine, pulled from another pocket. It was something he usually used in poppet work, for bindings. But better than a poppet was the real thing.

"You know—" He coughed. Cleared his throat. "You know what this is?" He knew she knew, but some things were better said aloud anyway.

Vizinha nodded.

Heath needed a moment to catch his breath before he could say enough to matter.

"Then you know I can bind you with it, and right now you couldn't stop me. I can bind away all your powers, then I can hide this away where you'll never find it. You won't be *mãe-de-santo* anymore. You'll just be you."

"You ... don't have it in you." She shook her head. "Not right now. You ... you're burnt out too."

"I have enough," Heath said, hoping it wasn't a bluff. "Don't make me prove it. Where is he?"

Vizinha hung her head forward and started crying.

"No," she said, and her words were plaintive. Weak. And worst of all, sincere. "Don't take him away."

"No choice," he said.

A hand on his shoulder. Heath whirled around too slow to stop anything, but it was just Tony, his flaming sword gone now. The monk's black clothes were ripped and torn, and he had cuts on his face, hands, and neck. Still, he stood steady. His eyes unclouded.

Colin stood behind Tony, and Colin looked about half-dead. Sopping with sweat and dragging every bit as much as Heath was.

"You won't need your cord," Tony said. "Go into the house and find the avatar. Take Colin with you. I will watch Vizinha."

Heath looked back at Vizinha, who was weeping quietly into her hands.

"You sure?" Heath asked Tony.

"Trust me," Tony said, and his voice sounded steady. Maybe even stronger than before, despite his wounds, and that just wasn't fair. "She needs to hear what I have to say."

Heath wasn't all that sure Vizinha had much of a soul left to save, but he was just too spent to argue the point.

"Come on," he said to Colin, and led the way into her house.

———

THE FRONT DOOR WAS UNLOCKED, WHICH SAVED HEATH THE embarrassment of having to go back for a key. As he opened the front door, Colin said, "I'll start in the basement. You start in the attic. First to find him hollers."

"No need," Heath said. "Come on."

Vizinha's house looked very *Better Homes and Gardens*. Stylishly decorated, not cluttered, and Heath suspected that each stick of furniture cost more than all of his furniture combined (save his bed).

He didn't have any attention to spare for the details, though he did note that her house smelled like ground herbs, same as his did. Right now he picked out more lemon verbena and star anise than anything else, but he had the feeling the scents changed on a daily basis, just like his place.

Heath led Colin up a pale wood stairway, decorated with paintings of Brazil that looked like original oil works.

Just how much did Vizinha charge? Maybe Nariko *did* have a point about Heath's rates. Even his recent increase seemed to leave him behind the curve.

They weren't at the top of the stairs before they heard a rich, baritone voice call out to them.

"Hello? Please. I need help."

Short hall at the top of the stairs, with a green and yellow runner rug. One closed door, and one open, and it was from the open doorway that the voice was coming.

"Please. I'm in here."

Heath reached the doorway of a bedroom done in pinks and whites. White chest of drawers with gold fixtures. The top held colorful decorative boxes, hangers for necklaces, a large jewelry case, and a single, white, porcelain unicorn.

The carpeting was white. The king size, four-poster bed had a pink comforter and frilly fringe on the decorative pillows.

And lying in the middle of the decorative pillows was a man who looked as though he should have been on the cover of a romance novel. He wore only black silk boxers and a black silk robe, currently hanging open. Not a hair on his tanned, muscled chest, or his smooth, chiseled jaw. He had short brown hair, neatly trimmed, and the kind of build that needed daily workouts to maintain.

The man's right hand was handcuffed to the bedpost.

Colin gave a long, slow whistle, and Heath wasn't sure if Colin was whistling at the man or the room. If Heath had whistled, it would have been at the room. It was the last thing he expected from Vizinha. More like bouncy sorority girl than seductive femme fatale, and not a single nod to her native homeland.

But Heath didn't have time for the décor.

"Your opposite number sent us," Heath said. "She's worried sick about you."

"Is she here?" He sat up and Colin almost started drooling again. "I thought I sensed her, but I couldn't be sure."

"No." Heath approached the handcuffs. Damn it, he needed his...

Heath's spirit eyes opened.

He instantly focused hard on the handcuffs and the magic binding this poor American Avatar of Male Sexuality to Vizinha's bed. The last thing Heath wanted to do was see this guy's real form, especially if it turned out to be the case that he had some homosexual tendencies he didn't know about.

He didn't think he did, but that would have been a hell of a way to discover them.

The spell work was solid, but simple. It was keyed into…

Heath looked around him — careful to keep the bound man out of his view — and sure enough, the handcuffs were keyed to spells woven into the walls of this room and…

A quick glance told Heath that the closet door continued the spells, but not the closet, while the spells did continue into the bathroom…

Which was also white, with pink trim.

"How long was she planning this?" He muttered.

"What?" Colin said, having to drag his attention away from the guy, which suggested that Heath's little *lust-dampener* was wearing off.

"This." Heath gestured to the walls, the decorating scheme, even the unicorn. "It's all part of the spell. The all-American bedroom to contain the perfect all-American man."

"What good does that do us?" Colin asked. "I'm in no shape to break spells this strong, and neither are you."

"No," Mr. Perfect said. "You can't leave me here."

Heath slammed his spirit eyes shut, then looked at the man on the bed.

"Don't worry," Heath said, firing off a quick text message. "We're not leaving you here."

"Heath," Colin started, but Heath spoke over him.

"Like this, Colin." He turned to Mr. Perfect. "Can you give us a hand moving the bed? We're pretty wiped out."

"Can't," Mr. Perfect said, and even Heath envied the rich smoothness of the man's baritone. "I can't even pull against the cuff or try to break the bedpost."

Heath sighed. "It's you and me then, Colin."

Colin gave up arguing with a mighty shrug.

Heath and Colin began heaving the bed by the bedpost Mr. Perfect was cuffed to. Mr. Perfect couldn't help them, but he at least got off the bed so they weren't pulling him too.

God, but that bed was heavy. They'd yanked it maybe all of a foot

— knocking over a small nightstand, covered with a frilly pink cloth and an old-fashioned wind-up clock — before Colin stopped them.

"This is stupid," he said. He started shoving the thick pillow-top mattress off the bed.

That, it turned out, Mr. Perfect could help with. With his muscle to aid them the mattress practically flew off of the bed frame.

The dragging went much faster now. Soon Heath was pulling and Colin pushing as the bedpost and its handcuff broke the plane of the doorway. Only an inch or two into the hallway, but apparently it was enough.

"Yes!" Mr. Perfect roared. One flex of his arm and the handcuff chain snapped. "Free!"

He struck a pose. Probably couldn't help it. Colin certainly appreciated the sight.

Heath shook his head and led the way out.

HEATH, COLIN AND MR. PERFECT WERE ONLY JUST EXITING VIZINHA'S house when Goldilocks came running down the driveway. Hershel ran right alongside her, some kind of 9mm pistol in his right hand.

Mr. Perfect ran to meet Goldilocks' embrace, while Vizinha whimpered. The two avatars spun in a circle as they kissed, and Heath couldn't help a welling feeling of satisfaction, watching them like that. It was like he was watching the end of a romantic comedy with Nariko, when the hero and heroine finally came together. As though it should have been followed by a cut to the two of them getting married, or going on a world cruise or something.

Vizinha started crying again, and Heath realized she was sitting in one of the wooden chairs on her porch. Tony sat in the other, smiling at the reunited perfect couple.

When the kiss finally broke, Mr. Perfect was about to say something, but Goldilocks spoke first and thunder underwrote her words.

"Where is she?"

Spotted Vizinha in a moment, then Goldilocks was running

again. From the expression on her face, she looked ready to tear Vizinha apart with her bare hands. And truth to tell, Heath wasn't feeling too inclined to stop her.

Tony felt differently.

The monk stood in front of Vizinha like a shield. Serene look on his face.

"No," he said, simply.

"Get out of my way," Goldilocks said. "I don't want to hurt you."

"Then don't. But don't hurt her either. Your perfect mate has been freed. Go. Enjoy your reunion and leave this matter to an even higher authority than yourself. There will be no murder here today."

"Damn it," Heath said with a sigh. Why did Tony have to use the m-word? Heath didn't have much of anything left, but he knew what he had to do.

He trudged to stand next to Tony.

"You paid me to get your man back. We did that. As for the rest, I told you. I can't condone murder."

"Please," Mr. Perfect said, putting a hand on Goldilocks' shoulder, making her sigh. "I just want to leave this place."

Goldilocks nodded. The perfect couple looked into each other's eyes for a moment, then both were smiling as they turned away. Walking with their arms around one another.

It wasn't a sunset they were walking into. It was just the light of a motion-sensor flood lamp. Even if that light looked unaccountably orange, with a flare of yellow around the bulb.

Hershel stepped up to Heath.

"I'll bring her final payment in the morning," he said, then grinned. "At a reasonable hour."

"Bless you," Heath said, with more relief in his voice than he was proud of.

Then all three American avatars were just ... gone. And the flood-light was glaring fluorescent blue-white again.

"You should go inside," Tony said to Vizinha. "Think about what I said. If you want to talk, you know where to reach me."

Vizinha didn't nod. Didn't acknowledge Tony's words at all, except to get up and go into her house, without so much as a glance back at Heath, Tony, or Colin.

"She should never have slept with him," Tony said softly. "Especially when he wasn't in control of himself. I hope she can recover from that."

Heath doubted Vizinha was going to change after this. Hell, he wouldn't have been shocked if her sadness were a show to get them to go away.

But just in that moment, Heath was too wiped out to care.

13

WHEN HEATH LATER THOUGHT BACK ON THE WALK FROM VIZINHA'S front porch to Colin's car, he was amazed he had enough strength to carry his backpack. He'd barely had enough strength to carry himself, much less anything else. He wrote it off to the power of habit. Either way, at a rate somewhere between a stumble and a trudge, Heath and Colin made it back across the street and into Colin's car.

Tony, well, he didn't quite vanish, but he came pretty close. He hovered a bit to make sure Heath and Colin made it to the Saturn — and Heath thought he remembered a brief conversation wherein Tony made sure Colin was okay to drive — but then the monk was just gone.

Though admittedly, the moment the door of Colin's Saturn closed, Heath didn't notice anything but the silence. Colin sat in the driver's seat next to him, but Heath couldn't even hear them breathing. Just a comforting lull. Or maybe it was just the sudden realization that, for the moment at least, no one was trying to kill him.

Either way, Heath wasn't aware of any sounds at all until Colin popped open the center console to hand him a wet nap.

Heath stared at the wet nap, then blinked at Colin.

"You've got some, uh, blood on your face."

Heath pulled down the vanity mirror.

Seemed that Vizinha hadn't been the only one bleeding from her nose, eyes, and ears.

Heath needed two wet naps for his face, then another for his hands. Colin just rested in the driver's seat until Heath said, "I can just take the MAX—"

"No," Colin said, starting the car. "I'll get you home."

It wasn't even ten o'clock on a Friday evening. Portland was hopping. Traffic everywhere, people going to restaurants, bars, clubs, coffee houses and more. But Colin's driving magic held, and traffic parted for Colin like the Red Sea did for Moses.

Heath was exhausted enough that he started laughing at the comparison. Colin started laughing too, his snicker less energetic that usual, though that might have been because he didn't know why they were laughing.

"What do you think?" Heath said at last. "If the Pharaoh's men were pursuing us, would Portland traffic crash down and crush them like the Red Sea did?"

"You need sleep worse than I do."

Colin was right. Heath didn't even try to make conversation the rest of the way, and after Colin dropped him off, Heath just wandered back toward his house, accompanied by the loud barking of all the neighborhood dogs.

That couldn't have been right, though. The neighborhood dogs were good dogs. Not the kind to bark all night. They only barked like that when...

Someone was standing on Heath's front porch.

Drake.

DRAKE DIDN'T LOOK LIKE DRAKE. DRAKE WAS SUPPOSED TO BE A sloppy, fat man with a receding hairline. The man standing on Heath's front porch was portly enough, sure, but that receding black hair was slicked down and styled like a fashion statement.

And the clothes. Charcoal gray silk shirt. Long-sleeved. Buttoned to just below the collar. Black pants, but they looked like quality suit material. Might've been silk themselves. Black polished dress shoes. Subtle belt with a touch of gold for the buckle.

Silver necklace. Goat's head pentagram thing. Single gold ring on the middle finger of each hand. Both looked to be engraved, it Heath could have mustered the attention and interest to notice the details.

"Heath Cyr—" Drake started, but Heath spoke anyway.

"Son of a bitch," Heath said. "Vizinha was right. You clean up pretty good."

"Heath Cyr—" Drake tried again, but Heath just kept right on talking.

"Look, man. I just got back from giving Vizinha the ass-whooping of the year. All I really want to do is go to sleep. So don't make me spank you like a bad little boy."

"Just give me the knife," Drake said, holding out his hand.

"The fuck should I?" Heath said, trying to make his words sound harsh instead of exhausted, but he had no sense of how well his effort worked out. "It's my insurance policy."

"Give it to me or—"

"You gonna stand there on my front porch and threaten me? *Sean Aaron Martinson?*" Heath started laughing while Drake turned scarlet. "Man, I *know* you have enough going for you to sense my guardian spirits. Long as I hold this knife," — Heath patted his backpack — "not to mention your true name, my guardians can cut through whatever you've got for ... what do you guys call them? Shields?"

"All right. All right." Drake held up his hands. "If I lay it all on the line, will you listen?"

Heath rolled his hand in a keep-it-moving gesture.

"My brother. You call him Tony. He gave me that knife for my twelfth birthday. I never go anywhere without it."

Heath let his silence say everything it needed to.

"I know," Drake said, "I *know*. That's what makes it so valuable. And I know you don't have any reason to do me any favors. So, what do I have to do to get it back?"

There's an old rule in negotiating. Old as time itself. It gets phrased a lot of ways, but the way Heath first heard it was, "the first side to name a number loses."

Heath had something valuable. Extremely valuable, given the state of relations between himself and Drake. The question wasn't what Heath wanted for it. The question was what would Drake offer to get it back?

"Money?" Drake tried, but Heath just raised an eyebrow in an are-you-kidding-me expression.

Drake tried to play silent for a moment, but Drake had two things going against him here. One, he desperately wanted the knife back, and two, Heath wasn't much more than half conscious, and had no problem looking bored and aloof about the whole discussion.

Drake broke first.

"Fine," he said. "I didn't want to do this, but if it's the only way. I will hand-write, in my own blood, a permission slip that lets anything you do — or any spirit acting at your instruction — right through my wards and shields, conditional to my—"

"Aren't any conditions on this knife or your name," Heath said.

"Too much," Drake said with a shake of his head. "Forget it."

"Fine," Heath said. "Then get the hell off my front porch and—"

"All right." Drake's head sagged forward and his tone sounded so defeated that Heath almost felt guilty. Almost. "No conditions. Note handwritten by me, in my own blood, letting your spells and spirits right through my wards."

"And what else?" Heath said. He knew he was pushing, but he was still pissed at Drake for that display at Gripper, not to mention the whole trying-to-kill-him thing.

"What else could you possibly want?"

"Money."

"Money?"

The sneer in Drake's voice upped the amount Heath was willing to accept.

"Look," Heath said with a sigh. "I realize you expect that my having unfettered magical access to your person is some great joy to me, but I really don't give a damn about you. I could happily live the rest of my life never interacting with you again, and whether it's your knife or your note, I want insurance *you're* never going to bug *me* again."

"Then—"

"I'm not finished." Heath needed to breathe a moment after the effort of that much snap in his voice. "But you, you son of a bitch, you've put me through a whole lot of hassle I didn't need, and you did it at a very bad time. Seems only right to me that you should pay for that."

"How much did you have in mind?" Drake said.

"Let me put it this way," Heath said with a smile. "How much do you think your enemies would bid for this knife, if I were to offer it up for auction."

Drake blanched. "You wouldn't."

"Be a quick and easy way to get you out of my life. Wouldn't it?"

Drake named a number much bigger than anything Heath had in mind. Heath made him double it anyway. Nariko would want him to, and besides, the guy was driving a freaking Ferrari. He could afford it.

"Fine." Drake shook his head. "Will you take a check?"

"I'll take cash, and you can bring it when you bring the note. *Then*, I'll give you your knife back."

"All right," Drake said with a sigh. "Tomorrow afternoon all right?"

Yes. Yes it was.

14

HEATH AWOKE LATE THE NEXT MORNING TO THE BEST SOUND HE'D heard in days: Nariko's knock. No mistaking it. She had a rhythmic, three-beat knock that started heavy on the first thump, and lightened each of the next two.

When Heath heard it, his eyes snapped open. He was lying on his belly, facing the mouse-tainted breath of his tuxedo cat, Dr. John, who was lying beside him on the rumpled sheets.

"Where did you find a mouse?" Heath muttered as he worked his way to a sitting position, accompanied by a symphony of popping, complaining joints.

That fight with Vizinha must have really taken it out of him.

Heath was still in last night's clothes. Short-sleeved red-and-white striped shirt with buttons. Khaki cargo shorts. At least he must have dropped his backpack and kicked off his boat shoes. That was something. And the clock on his nightstand said it was about eleven, which meant close to twelve hours sleep.

So why did his mouth taste like stale beer?

Nariko's knock came again.

Heath was on his feet and moving before he knew it. Moving

better than last night, too. Feet actually walking, instead of stumbling or trudging. Definite improvement.

When he opened the door, Nariko leapt right into his arms, bowling them both over and into his big leather recliner. She was wearing a cream-colored tank top and cut-off jeans shorts and looked like an ad for sex appeal.

"I like the way you think," she said, snuggling for a moment and starting for a kiss before pulling back, "but whew! What died in your mouth?"

"Beer," Heath said. "I—"

He gave up when Nariko pointed him toward the bathroom. She followed along, smiling as he brushed his teeth and rinsed his mouth, and generally replaced the taste of stale beer with the fresher taste of mint.

"Better?" he asked, going for a kiss but meeting an objecting finger.

"Much," she said, one eyebrow raised high. "But only one kiss before you've got some explaining to do."

Heath made the most of that kiss. Tried to tell Nariko just exactly how much he missed her and take his time doing it. For her part, she must have missed him just as much, to judge by that kiss, and the little way she hummed before finally pulling back.

"Naughty boy," she said. "Trying to get me worked up enough to forget my explanation?"

"I just thought explanations always sounded better naked and post-coital," Heath said in a low tone.

"Tempting," she said, "but not just yet. Think of it as foreplay, if it helps."

Nariko pulled out of his arms and sauntered back down the hall toward the kitchen. Watching her walk away, Heath found the foreplay comparison more apt than he expected.

Soon the two of them were sitting at his kitchen table, basking in the warm, natural light and sipping coffee.

"So," Nariko said at last. "On the way back from the airport, Colin told me all about the last few days. Especially last night. Drake. Vizinha. Mr. Perfect. So, let's start with the two most important questions. One, where do you get off, not telling me about a serious death threat?"

"But—"

"No 'buts.'" Her tone was light enough, but those emerald eyes of hers darkened as though a storm brewed on the horizon. "Let's get something straight. If this is going to work, you can't hide that kind of thing from me. Understand?"

"Can I talk?"

Nariko nodded as she sipped her coffee.

"I did tell you."

"No," she said, setting her mug down firmly. "You said he 'declared war.' And you said he 'wanted to kill you.' Not that same thing as saying, 'Nari, Drake decreed my death in front of a packed house at Gripper.'"

Heath blinked. He was sure he'd come clean. Nariko must have misinterpreted the blink though, because she sighed.

"If it's a private thing," she said, as though Heath needed the explanation, "you slap his hand hard enough and he'll go away. What he did though put everything on the line..."

Heath's breath caught as realization spread through him. He *had* held back. Apparently this complete honesty thing was going to be harder than he thought.

"You're right," he said. "I held back key information. And I shouldn't have. Much like you shouldn't have held back about your trip."

"We'll get to me," Nariko said, and that storm building in her eyes looked a little further away. "I promise. You're going first, though. And I'm not happy to hear you threatening to make zombies either. That's your uncle's thing."

"You're part of it though," Heath said, then sighed and leaned back in his chair. "I knew you were doing something big. Didn't know exactly how dangerous, but I had a pretty good guess going. And a death threat from Drake, well, it didn't seem like anything I couldn't handle myself. Certainly nothing I wanted to see split your focus when you were doing something dangerous."

Nariko grimaced. "Fair enough. But next time, tell me. Even if you don't think you need my help. Even if you think it might split my focus." She reached out and poked Heath in the chest three times. "You. Tell. Me. Clear?"

"Clear," Heath said, "as long as it works both ways."

"We'll get to me."

She crossed her heart, and Heath tried not to be distracted by where the gesture led his eyes. It was as though all the pent up sexual desire he wasn't feeling around Goldilocks was coming crashing down on him here and now.

"Eyes up here, baby," Nariko said softly, but there was a smile trying to make its way onto her lips. "For a while, anyway."

Heath looked up at her.

"Now, the big one," Nariko said, and that storm front in her eyes was back on the approach. "We had a plan. You were going to wait for me to go after Vizinha. Now you gave Colin some bullshit line about Vizinha being distracted or not home or some other excuse to pretend last night was the perfect time.

Nariko shook her head, her long black hair dancing about her shoulders. "I want the real reason you took that big a risk. Did something that stupid, when you've said yourself I'm the heaviest hitter you know. And Heath, your reason better be a good one."

"It's stupid," he muttered.

"Granted," Nariko said without missing a beat. "But I want to hear it anyway."

"I..." Heath shook his head and forced the words out. "I didn't want to see you meet Mr. Perfect."

That furrowed Nariko's brow and made her blink a few times.

"Why?" she said, honest puzzlement all through her voice. "Colin was positive nothing happened between you and Ms. Perfect, so it's not like I would have felt some magical compulsion to throw off my clothes and jump him."

"It's not that..."

"And Ms. Perfect had no trouble going the generic beauty route around you, so by the same logic, you wouldn't have to worry if my deep-seated fantasy man wasn't your identical twin."

"Just ... listen a second..."

Heath picked up his coffee, then set it back down without a sip. He slid his chair a little close to Nariko. Took her hands in his.

"You'd been gone for days. Fighting, for all I knew, and we both know how you get after a fight."

"And we both know I can control myself. It's not like I'm Colin."

"No. Of course not. It's just ... for all I knew you were going to come back with some seriously pent-up horniness, straight into another fight, followed by meeting the American Avatar of Male Sex Appeal. Mr. Perfect, he couldn't help but react to that. It's his nature."

Nariko raised an eyebrow, but let Heath finish.

"I ... I wasn't sure I could handle watching you react to *him*."

"But you had no problem around Ms. Perfect, and the two of you were alone together, more than once, after I'd been teasing you over video chat."

"And she told me why." Heath took a deep breath. Hoped she didn't notice his palms sweating. Why did his hands have to feel so clammy at a time like this? And why did the sun have to get so warm? He felt positively feverish.

"I love you, Nari," Heath said. "Not just words, but the real thing. Going way down deep. Even Ms. Perfect admitted she could have pulled out all the stops and still failed to seduce me. 'Cause she's just a fantasy. And I've ... I've got the real thing."

Heath wasn't sure what he expected, but it wasn't the softness that came into Nariko's voice then, or the shine that came into her eyes.

"And you thought..." she said.

"If I saw you react to Mr. Perfect..." Heath couldn't bring himself to finish the sentence.

Nariko slipped one hand free of his. Stroked Heath's cheek and shook her head just the barest bit.

"Dumb in all the wrong ways," she whispered.

Nariko stood, tugging Heath to his feet by the hand she still held.

"Where?" Heath asked as he stood, knees wobbly from how raw he felt, opening himself up the way he hadn't to anyone, maybe ever.

"Where do you think, dum-dum?" She smiled. "I can tell you I love you all day. But actions speak louder than words."

Nariko led Heath to the bedroom.

AFTERWARDS THEY LAY NAKED TOGETHER AMONG THE NOW HOPELESSLY rumpled sheets of Heath's bed, Nariko cooing to Dr. John as she scritched the cat's belly while his purr rumbled louder than a Harley Davidson.

The whole room smelled like what they'd been doing, and it was a good smell.

Heath felt more relaxed and content than he'd felt in a good, long while. Still...

Heath rolled up behind Nariko, and she snuggled into him as she continued scritching Dr. John's belly.

"You know," Heath started, but stopped speaking when she sighed.

"I know," she said. "So sue me if I wanted to be naked and post-coital when we got to my part of the day's confessions."

"I think you made the right call," Heath said, his smile as much in his voice as on his face.

"Mmmm," Nariko said, rolling onto her back. "You're sure round four doesn't sound better than—"

"Yes, but spill it anyway."

"Fine."

She pulled up to sit against the headboard, and Heath tried not to let himself get distracted by her naked glory. He knew he needed to hear what she had to say. So instead of lying there staring up at her or snuggling in, he slid up the sheets to sit next to her.

Dr. John, no longer being petted, leapt down in a huff.

Nariko looked off toward the bathroom as she spoke.

"I needed answers about my mom. I think you know I wasn't joking when I said she wasn't going to die."

"I never think you're joking about your mother."

Heath had paid special attention to the little things Nariko had let slip about her mother from time to time. Her power. Her age. And the idea that she might be immortal had come up more than once.

"I thought," Nariko said, "I thought she was just *bakemono*. Shifter spirit of sorts, if a powerful one, but every so often you'll hear about one falling in love with a human, like my dad." A sad half-smile curved her lips. "Romantic in a way, and it explained a little about my own power."

Heath had wondered from time to time about Nariko's power. He'd seen her pull off some serious stunts, especially while in touch with a mountain. But that might just have been consistent with her Shugendō practice, for all he knew.

"But lately..." She turned and looked Heath in the eye. "You've felt that spirit before, haven't you? The one in the hill under their house?"

"Yeah. Big thing. Sleeping, though."

"Not so much lately." She shook her head. "It's been stirring. And every time I've visited Mom and Dad lately, it's felt, well, serpentine."

"You don't mean—"

"Yes I do. I think maybe there's a dragon sleeping in a hill under Lake Oswego."

"What's that have to do with your mother?"

"Mom had been ... I don't know ... bouncier than usual. More energetic."

Heath tried to picture stoic Mrs. Tachibana acting bouncy, but couldn't manage it.

"Except with Dad," Nariko said. "She's been getting short with him. Impatient. And I, well, I started wondering. And I knew the only place I'd find answers was down around Mount Fuji, where my aunt and uncle live."

"Your dad's siblings or your mom's?"

"That's just it," Nariko said with a forced smile. "Neither. My sisters and I were raised to *think* they were mom's brother and sister, but I shattered that lie easily enough, so near to a mountain as ancient and powerful as Fuji."

"So what were they?"

"*They* were bakemono." Nariko sighed. "*Kitsune*, to be precise. Fox spirits, you'd call them. I got them to admit the truth."

Nariko closed her eyes and leaned back against the headboard.

"My mother is a mountain dragon. And I think my baby sister takes after her."

"But," Heath said carefully, "Japanese dragons are good, right? Not like those European treasure-hoarders?"

"Not that simple."

"So what does that mean for you?"

Her eyes still closed, she shook her head. "Don't know yet."

Heath pulled Nariko into his arms. Kissed each of her closed eyes one at a time, then a soft, gentle kiss on her lips.

"You're not going to face this alone," he whispered.

That got him a faint smile.

Someone knocked on the front door. Six heavy thumps.

Nariko's eyes were open and alert in an instant. "Company? Or trouble?"

"Money," Heath said, hopping off the bed to grab his red robe.

He was still tying the robe in place as he hustled down the hall to the hushing sound of his bare feet on the hardwood floor.

He opened the front door, and there stood Hershel, smile on the big man's face like he knew what Heath had been up to.

Hershel didn't say a word. Just handed Heath a thick white envelope, clapped him on the shoulder, and vanished.

Heath chose not to think about whether or not the American avatars were watching him as closely as the Lwa. Instead he grabbed two cups of coffee from the kitchen before he hustled back down the hall to Nariko.

"Bless you," she said, taking a cup and gratefully drinking in its strong, rich flavor.

"And that's not all." Heath tossed the envelope on her lap with a wide grin.

Nariko raised an eyebrow, set her coffee on the nightstand, and picked up the envelope.

"Giving a naked girl an envelope full of cash," she said, then gave him a sweet smile. "And honey, it's not nearly enough."

"For you? Not even close." He kissed her then took the envelope back and fanned through the many hundred dollar bills. "This was my fee for rescuing Mr. Perfect."

"Not bad," Nariko grudgingly admitted. "I'd have gotten you more though."

"But there's more coming."

Heath grinned broadly, so much pleasure in his expression that Nariko smiled just as wide.

"What?" she said.

"Let me tell you about coming home to find Drake on my doorstep."

Heath got Nariko laughing good and hard as he told the story with as much truth as it needed, and just enough embellishment to make it memorable.

And when he finished, even Nariko agreed he'd gotten enough money out of Drake.

SIGN UP FOR STEFON'S NEWSLETTER

Stefon loves to keep in touch with his readers, and loves to keep you reading. The best way for him to do both is for you to sign up for his newsletter.

Sign up at http://www.stefonmears.com/join

If you sign up for Stefon's newsletter, you get...

- Monthly updates about his publishing and travel schedules
- His latest news, in brief, and answers to reader questions
- A free short story for signing up
- List-only offers and occasional specials
- Plus a free short story every month!

ABOUT THE AUTHOR

Stefon Mears is not allowed to summon demons in the house. Stefon has more than thirty books to his credit, and he never stops writing. He earned his M.F.A. in Creative Writing from N.I.L.A., and his B.A. in Religious Studies (double emphasis in Ritual and Mythology) from U.C. Berkeley. He's a lifelong gamer and fantasy fan. Stefon lives in Portland, Oregon, with his wife and three cats.

Look for Stefon online:
www.stefonmears.com
himself@stefonmears.com

www.ingramcontent.com/pod-product-compliance
Lightning Source LLC
Chambersburg PA
CBHW050529190726
48284CB00003B/1004